THE MOSS FILE
AN AUNT BESSIE COLD CASE MYSTERY
BOOK THIRTEEN

DIANA XARISSA

Copyright © 2024 by DX Dunn, LLC

Cover Copyright © 2024 Tell-Tale Book Covers

ISBN: 9798324477677

All rights reserved.

No part of this publication may be reproduced, distributed, or transmitted in any form or by any means, including photocopying, recording, or other electronic or mechanical methods, without the prior written permission of the publisher, except as permitted by U.S. copyright law. For permission requests, contact diana@dianaxarissa.com

The story, all names, characters, and incidents portrayed in this production are fictitious. No identification with actual persons (living or deceased), places, buildings, and products is intended or should be inferred.

First edition 2024

❦ Created with Vellum

CHAPTER 1

"Bessie, hello," Marjorie Stevens said as Bessie tapped on her open office door. "Come in and have a seat."

Bessie walked into the office and sat at one of the comfortable chairs in front of the woman's desk. As she got settled, she noticed the nameplate on the desk.

"Senior archivist? Is that a promotion?" she asked the pretty blonde woman.

Marjorie shrugged. "I think Manx National Heritage just decided that I needed a new title. There isn't any junior archivist, and I'm still the librarian for the Manx Museum Library, but they are paying me a few extra pence for my efforts."

"I'm glad to hear that. You work very hard."

"I suppose so, but I love what I do. When I was younger, I often imagined how wonderful it would be to spend all of my time surrounded by old documents, just immersing myself in history. Don't tell anyone, but if they stopped paying me, I'd still come to work every day."

Bessie laughed. "You definitely don't want anyone to hear you saying that."

"It's so good to see you. I was worried that we'd upset you in some way, when you stopped coming in to see us, but then I found out about the cold case unit, and it all made sense."

"The cold case unit does keep me very busy."

"The article in the local paper said that you spend a fortnight each month considering a cold case."

Bessie nodded. "Some members of the unit only come to the island for a week at a time. Once we've had some initial discussions about the case, they can go back to London and work from there if necessary." *But so far we've solved every case while they've still been on the island*, she added silently. She wasn't supposed to talk about how successful they'd been.

"I hope you have time for a long chat. I want to hear all about the cold case unit and how it works. The man who started it is a former Scotland Yard detective, isn't he?"

"Yes, Andrew Cheatham worked for Scotland Yard in the homicide unit. He retired a few years ago."

"How did you even meet him?"

"Ah, that's a bit of a long story. Do you remember me talking about going across to a holiday park with my friend Doona Moore some years ago?"

Marjorie nodded. "I believe you've gone more than once."

"Yes, we have now, but we met Andrew on our first visit. Doona was told she'd won a holiday at the park in a contest."

"I do remember you telling me that. She was very excited about winning and she invited you to join her at the park."

"Exactly, but when we got there, we discovered that she hadn't actually won the holiday. Her estranged husband, who was part-owner of the park, had arranged for the holiday because he'd wanted to see her again."

Marjorie sighed. "Poor Doona."

"Sadly, the man was murdered before he and Doona had a chance to talk."

"This is all sounding vaguely familiar. There must have been some island gossip about all of this. Didn't Doona inherit a fortune from the man?"

"He did leave his entire estate to her. There were some life insurance policies, and he also left her small shares in various properties across the UK. The only thing that Doona kept was a share in the holiday park."

"Which explains why you keep going back."

Bessie nodded. "Doona goes back and forth quite a lot, actually. She spent a large part of the summer there, but she always comes back to the island for the cold case unit meetings."

"Of course, because she's part of the unit. I suppose that's why she quit working at the constabulary, then. When I heard she wasn't working there any longer, my first thought was that she's far too young to be retired."

Bessie grinned. "She's not quite fifty, so much too young to retire. I believe, if you ask her, that she'll tell you that managing the holiday park from here is a full-time job."

"And she was only a part-time receptionist at the constabulary. I did wonder if she found it awkward, working with Inspector John Rockwell after they'd become personally involved."

"I believe they both enjoyed working together, actually. Doona also helps John with the children, which takes up a lot of her time."

"Ah, those poor kids," Marjorie said. "Imagine your mother leaving your father for another man and then finding out that she never actually loved your father, that she was still in love with the other man, someone she'd been involved with years earlier."

"I'm not certain how much of the story they know," Bessie said, wondering why Marjorie knew so much of the story.

"It must have been a lot worse when their mother married the other man and then dumped them on the island with their father while she and her new husband went all the way to Africa for a very long honeymoon."

"I believe the children were happy to be left with John."

"Yes, of course, but then their mother passed away unexpectedly. That must have been dreadful for them."

Bessie nodded. "It was terribly sad. Thomas and Amy are doing great, though. John is a brilliant father and, as I said, Doona helps a great deal."

"As I understand it, Inspector Rockwell and Doona are very happy together."

"I believe so."

Marjorie shook her head. "But you were explaining how you met Inspector Cheatham."

"Was I?" Bessie laughed. "We have wandered off topic. It's quite simple, really. He was staying in the cottage next to where Doona and I were staying. When he discovered that we were involved in a police investigation, he offered to help."

"That was kind of him."

"He is very kind, but I think he was also quite bored at the holiday park and missing police work."

"I can understand that. I don't ever want to retire."

Bessie shrugged. "I've never held a paying job, so it's difficult for me to imagine giving one up."

"They are paying you to be on the cold case unit, though, aren't they?"

"We do get a stipend for the work that we do."

"But you received an inheritance when you were very young, didn't you? I remember you telling me about the man you loved and how he passed away on a sea journey to the island to come to see you."

Bessie swallowed the small lump in her throat that still appeared whenever she talked about Matthew Saunders. "Yes, Matthew and I met when I was living in the US. I was only seventeen, and when my parents decided to return to the island, they insisted that I return with them. We'd left the island when I was only two years old, and I didn't remember it at all. I wanted to stay in America and marry Matthew, but they wouldn't hear of it."

"And when he died, he left you everything he had."

"It wasn't a lot, but it was enough to allow me to buy my cottage on the beach so that I no longer had to live with my parents. I blamed them for Matthew's death. My advocate invested what was left and, by living very frugally, I never had to find work."

"And we've wandered off topic again," Marjorie laughed. "Tell me about Inspector Cheatham."

"As I said, he's been retired for years now. He has a large family with children, grandchildren, and great-grandchildren. His wife passed away years ago now. He has a flat in London, but he spends a fortnight each month on the island working with the cold case unit."

"Someone told me that he usually stays in one of the cottages on the beach near your cottage."

"He does. He likes being right on the water, and from there it isn't a long drive to Ramsey. We typically have our meetings at the Seaview, which is where the other members of the unit who come in from London usually stay when they're here."

"I'm trying to remember what I read about the other members," Marjorie said. "One of them is a homicide inspector, I believe."

"That's Harry Blake, but he's also retired."

"There were pictures in the paper. He looked rather unpleasant, really."

"He's not the least bit unpleasant, but he's also not terribly friendly, if that makes sense."

Marjorie nodded. "And the other inspector from London is an expert in missing persons, isn't he?"

"Charles Morris is one of the world's leading experts in finding missing people," Bessie said. "He's also retired, but he's in huge demand as a consultant. Harry does a lot of consultancy work, too, actually."

"I can see why they are both in the unit, then," Marjorie said. "And Inspector Rockwell is an excellent inspector who does a wonderful job policing Laxey and Lonan here on the island."

"He's very good at his job," Bessie agreed.

"And Doona used to work for the police, which is probably why she was asked to join the unit."

Bessie shook her head. "When Andrew was putting the unit together, he selected people that he knew could work well together to solve cases. John, Doona, Hugh, and I worked together to solve a lot of murders here on the island."

Marjorie shuddered. "There were quite a lot of murders in a very short space of time, weren't there? And you were involved in every case."

"Unfortunately."

"But you helped solve them all, which is the most important thing. And even better, there hasn't been a murder on the island in over a year."

"Thankfully."

"I'd forgotten that young Hugh Watterson is a part of the cold case unit. He's just a constable, isn't he?"

"He is, but he's taking classes at night, working towards a degree. He wants to be an inspector one day."

"Good for him, but when does he sleep? He and his wife have a small child, don't they?"

"They do, and Aalish is getting a little brother or sister in February."

"How exciting for them, but also how exhausting."

Bessie nodded. "Hugh manages to fit it all in. The constabulary gives him time off to be part of the cold case unit, which helps."

"The newspaper article hinted that the unit has had some success."

"We have had some success, but I can't really talk about anything that we do."

"I read in the London papers recently about a cold case there. After five years, the police had finally worked out who killed three people at a Christmas party at a London hotel."

"I read about that, too," Bessie said.

Marjorie raised an eyebrow. "Did you, now?"

"We look at cases from all over the world, and they aren't all murder investigations, either."

"And you aren't going to tell me if you solved the London hotel case or not, are you?"

"I suppose you're wondering why I'm here," Bessie said.

"And she changes the subject. I'm going to assume that your unit solved that case, then. Otherwise, you would have just denied any involvement."

"Someone asked me about the name of my cottage."

Marjorie laughed. "Okay, no more about the cold case unit, then. What about the name of your cottage?"

"It's 'Treoghe Bwaane,'" Bessie told her.

"'Widow's Cottage' in Manx. I can understand why you chose that name."

"But that's just it. I didn't choose the name. It was already called Treoghe Bwaane when I bought it. Someone recently asked me why, which made me realise that I don't know."

Marjorie frowned. "I'm surprised that you never did any research into the history of your own cottage. You've spent so much time in our archives doing research into so many things."

"Perhaps oddly, I never really thought about it. I suppose when I first bought the cottage, I was so devastated to have lost Matthew that I wasn't thinking clearly. Over time, the name just became part of the cottage and I never thought to question it."

"And now you're questioning it."

"Now I'm curious. I'd love to find out more, but I'm not certain I can. I should have asked my neighbours on the beach about it when I first moved in, but I barely spoke to anyone in those days."

"I would imagine they're all gone now," Marjorie said thoughtfully.

Bessie nodded. "Thomas and Maggie Shimmin started buying cottages on the beach about twenty years ago, with a plan to replace them with holiday cottages once they owned them all. It took them years to acquire every property on the beach, aside from mine, but once they'd managed it, they tore them all down and built the holiday cottages that are there now."

"And none of the former residents are still on the island?" Marjorie asked.

"Most of them passed away, and their heirs sold the cottages to Thomas and Maggie. A few moved into care homes elsewhere on the island, but the last of my former neighbours passed away more than a year ago."

"How long have you lived in the cottage?"

Bessie frowned. She didn't like to think about her age. "More than sixty years," she said eventually.

"Do you still have the paperwork from the sale of the

house? That would have the name of the previous owner on it."

"I don't believe I have any of that paperwork, but I'm certain my advocate must."

"That might be the best place to start. Of course, we have Woods' Atlas. That collection of maps was put together in 1867 by James Woods and might be able to tell you who owned the land at that time."

Bessie nodded. "I should have thought of that myself."

"It's probably best to start with the most recent owners and work backwards. The *Libri Vastarum* is all on microfilm if you want to work your way through it."

"That's the book that records changes of ownership, isn't it?"

"It is, but it isn't completely indexed. You're probably better off starting with your advocate and working from there. Once you have a name, you can search the parish registers for more information about the owners."

"I'll talk to Breesha today."

"While you're getting that name, I'll have a look through Woods' Atlas and see what I can find. I'll also look through our archive catalogues and see if I can find any reference to Treoghe Bwaane."

"You have catalogues?"

"We're working on them. I have a team of students from the local college working in the archives with me. They've been going through everything and trying to catalogue more of our holdings. You know that we have boxes and boxes of documents and old papers from across the island. They're a wonderful resource, but they're useless as long as no one knows what is actually in them."

Bessie knew exactly what Marjorie meant, because she herself had spent some time cataloguing boxes of old papers for the museum. As a strictly amateur historian, Bessie had spent years studying wills and other old documents. Her job with the cold case unit had meant that it had been quite some time since she'd done any work with the museum, though.

"Please let me know if you find anything," Bessie said. "I'll see if I can get a name from Doncan."

"When you do, ring me and let me know what you've found. I can get one of my assistants to search the parish registers for Laxey for you."

"I don't want to give you more work to do. I can search the registers myself."

"When is your next cold case meeting?"

Bessie sighed. "Andrew and the others are flying across tomorrow morning. The unit will meet in the afternoon."

"And then you'll be busy for a fortnight."

"Maybe not a fortnight, but certainly for a week."

"It's up to you," Marjorie said. "Of course, you're welcome to do the research yourself, but I have assistants who can help while you're busy with the cold case unit."

"Let me see what I can get from Doncan. I can decide from there."

"And while you're doing that, I'll see if we have anything in the archives that might be of interest. I know we got a dozen or more boxes from an old house in Laxey that was about to be torn down. The attic was full of boxes of old papers, which we were happy to take. I don't know that there will be anything useful to you in them, but you never know."

"I know which house you mean. It was a large property right on Laxey Harbour, so quite near to my cottage. I suppose it's possible that there was some connection between the family that owned the house and the owners of my cottage."

"Oh, I do hope so," Marjorie said. "I'm almost as eager as you are to find out who named your cottage and why."

Bessie chuckled. "I think it's a bit optimistic to think we'll be able to find out that much."

"How old was the cottage when you bought it?"

Marjorie grabbed a pen and a notebook and looked at Bessie expectantly.

"I'm not certain, but it had been there for some time, maybe fifty years, maybe more."

"So there might have been several previous owners, and any one of them might have named the cottage."

Bessie nodded. "And we may not be able to learn much about any of them."

"I shall have a think about other resources in the archives that might help. Ring me when you have a name for the previous owner."

"I will, and thank you for your help."

Bessie stood up and then, after Marjorie got up too, gave the woman a hug.

"And come and visit me more often," Marjorie said as she walked Bessie out of the office and down the corridor. "You know you're always welcome."

"I know, but I feel quite guilty coming here when I'm not here to work."

"You worked very hard for us for many years, and now you work very hard for Scotland Yard. I'm just proud to tell people that I know you."

Bessie shook her head at the thought. "I'll ring you soon," she promised as Marjorie opened the large wooden exit door.

"Please do."

There were a dozen stone steps from the doorway to the car park. When Bessie reached the ground, she turned and began a slow stroll back towards the centre of Douglas.

"And since I'm in the neighbourhood, I might as well go and visit Doncan rather than ringing him," she decided.

A short while later, she was sitting comfortably across a desk from Breesha, Doncan's assistant, with a cup of tea and a small plate of biscuits in front of her.

"Before you arrived, I was just looking for an excuse to take a break and have a biscuit or two," Breesha told Bessie. "I'm ever so glad you're here."

Bessie laughed. "You don't even know what I want."

"That's very true, but once I've had a cuppa and a biscuit, I'll be ready for anything."

The pair chatted about the unseasonably cold weather they'd been having since late September.

"I do hope it improves before Hop-tu-Naa," Bessie said. "I hate to imagine the children going door-to-door when it's so cold."

Breesha nodded. "We've over a fortnight to go before Hop-tu-Naa, though. I'm sure the weather will improve by then. But what brings you in today? I do hope that nothing is wrong."

"Nothing is wrong. I've just been wondering about my cottage, that's all."

"Wondering about your cottage?"

"Wondering about its name. It's called 'Treoghe Bwaane,' which is Manx for 'Widow's Cottage.' I've been wondering why it was given that name."

Breesha frowned. "Do you think Doncan or his father might know?"

"I doubt it, but I was hoping you might still have the paperwork from when I bought the cottage. That would at least give me the name of the sellers."

"Ah, and then you can do some research and see what you can find."

"Exactly."

"When did you buy the cottage?" As soon as she asked the question, Breesha flushed.

Everyone who knew Bessie knew that she was sensitive about her age.

"Never mind that, it will all be in your file," Breesha said quickly. "The problem is, a lot of the older files aren't kept here any longer. They're all safe enough, but they're kept in a storage unit in Jurby. There isn't enough space here for all of the paperwork that multiple generations of advocates have generated."

"Advocates are rather fond of paperwork."

"You can say that again," Breesha said, glancing at the pile of papers beside her on the desk.

"Does that mean that you can't help me?"

"Oh, no. Of course I'll help, but it may take a few days. I'll need to drive up to Jurby and then go through dozens of old filing cabinets until I find the right one. I'll talk to Doncan later today to see when he can spare me this week or next. I'll ring you as soon as I have any information."

"I didn't mean to cause you so much bother."

"It's no bother at all. I'm quite pleased to have a chance to get away from my desk for a day, anyway. Digging through old files in Jurby sounds almost as if it will be a holiday."

They talked for a short while longer before Breesha's phone rang. As she reached for it, Bessie gathered up her things.

"Thank you," she said quickly.

"I'll ring you," Breesha promised before she picked up the receiver.

CHAPTER 2

"Good morning, Bessie," Andrew said the next morning after Bessie opened the door to his knock.

"Good morning," she replied. "Welcome back to the island."

He grinned. "It's good to be back."

Bessie concentrated on keeping a smile on her face as she studied her friend. She knew that Andrew had some health concerns, and that his doctors were planning an operation for him in the near future, but she was still shocked to see how pale and unwell he looked.

"Did Helen come with you again?" she checked. Helen was Andrew's daughter. She'd been travelling to the island with her father most months now, ever since his doctors had decided that he shouldn't be on his own. One of her brothers had made the trip once, but otherwise, Helen had been making the journey.

Andrew nodded. "And she says I'm looking quite unwell these days," he replied. "I suppose you'll agree with her."

"You are a bit pale," Bessie said diplomatically. "I'm sure the sea air will help."

"It always does. I always feel much better when I'm on the island than when I'm in London."

"Even when we're struggling with a seemingly impossible cold case?"

Andrew chuckled. "We've solved them all, haven't we? No matter how difficult they seem, we always manage to find a solution in the end."

"Which is surprising, considering your expectations when we started."

He nodded. "I didn't think we'd solve more than ten per cent of the cases we considered. In some ways, that might have been easier. With every case we solve, I feel more pressure to solve the next one."

"We're going to fail at some point," Bessie said. "We have to be ready for that failure."

"It won't be this month. This month's case should have been solved years ago."

"Oh?"

"And I'm not saying another word. We're meeting in just a few hours. I'll tell you, and everyone else, all about the case then."

"That's fair enough. Do you want to get some lunch before the meeting?"

"I do, but first I need to rest for a short while. Flying is hard work."

"And your arms get tired," Bessie suggested.

Andrew laughed. "I'll be back around midday. We can drive to the Seaview and have lunch there if that suits you."

"That sounds good."

Bessie watched as the man slowly walked back towards the first holiday cottage in the row. He nearly always stayed in that cottage when he came for the cold case unit meetings.

She waited until he was safely inside his temporary home before she closed her door.

"He's going to be fine," she told herself as she walked back into her sitting room. "He's just tired from the journey."

She read for a short while and then got ready for lunch. When the kitchen clock showed quarter past twelve, she made her way over to Andrew's cottage.

"Hello, Bessie." Helen greeted her with a hug.

"Andrew was going to meet me at midday," Bessie told her. "We were going to get lunch at the Seaview before the meeting."

Helen frowned. "He's asleep, and I'd rather not wake him. He hasn't been sleeping very well at home."

"That's fine. I can make myself a sandwich for lunch. Are you going to wake him in time for the cold case unit meeting?"

"I suppose I'm going to have to, even though I'd rather not. He'll be cross enough with me for letting him miss lunch, though. He'd never forgive me if I let him miss a unit meeting."

"What time do you intend to wake him?"

"Half one."

"Do you want me to come back over at half one so that I'm here and ready to go when he's ready?"

"You could. He'll be far less grumpy with me if he knows you're here."

"I can't imagine your father being grumpy."

Helen laughed. "You've only seen him on his best behaviour. He can be incredibly grumpy when things don't go his way. As he continues to struggle with his health, he's getting grumpier as well."

"I am sorry."

"Thank you. He'll be better while he's here. He loves the

island. He knows the cold case unit is making a real difference. And he enjoys spending time with you."

"I enjoy his company, too."

Helen nodded. "You're more than welcome to stay and have lunch with me. I hired my own car this time so that I don't have to work around my father's schedule every day. He came straight here from the airport, but I stopped for groceries. I have everything you could possibly want in a sandwich. I never know what will sound good to my father, so I bought a little bit of everything."

"I don't want to eat your food."

"Please, eat. I bought more than enough for the two of us for a week. Nothing will keep longer than that. I will have to go shopping again at least one more time while we're here."

Bessie hesitated. "I don't want to be in your way."

"I was just sitting and watching television. I took the day off from work today because we were travelling. I'll work extra hard tomorrow to make up for it."

"How is working from here going?"

"It's an interesting challenge, but everyone at my company is very understanding. Last month I felt as if I spent the entire fortnight on the telephone in conference calls and meetings. This month I've brought a few projects with me that I can work on from here. That should be better than the endless phone calls."

"It sounds better, anyway."

The pair were eating sandwiches with salads, crisps, and fizzy drinks when Andrew walked into the room an hour later.

"Bessie, we were going to go to the Seaview," he said.

"But then Helen invited me to lunch, and I couldn't resist," Bessie replied.

Andrew frowned. "You should have woken me when Bessie arrived," he told Helen.

"I thought you needed the sleep," she said.

Andrew sighed. "You aren't wrong, but I am sorry that Bessie was disappointed."

"I'm not the least bit disappointed. The Seaview will always be there, but I don't often get to spend time with Helen. She's been telling me stories from her childhood."

"I hope she's been kind about me," Andrew said.

"Mostly," Bessie told him with a laugh.

Andrew made himself a sandwich and then joined them at the table. The trio chatted easily together until it was time for Bessie and Andrew to head to Ramsey.

"I am sorry about lunch," Andrew said as he drove them towards the Seaview.

"I truly don't mind. I enjoyed Helen's company, and you clearly needed the sleep."

"I don't sleep well in London, and then I come here and the sea air makes me feel so much better."

"Perhaps, after your surgery, you should recuperate over here."

"That's a thought. I shall have to talk to my doctors about my options."

A short while later, he pulled into the large car park for the Seaview Hotel.

"Maybe I could stay here while I recuperate," he said as he and Bessie got out of his hire car.

"It's a beautiful hotel."

"It certainly is."

They slowly crossed the car park. Bessie did her best to match her pace to Andrew's, a pace that felt incredibly slow to her.

Inside the large foyer, Andrew stopped. "I never get tired of this space," he said.

Bessie looked around and nodded. "Stuart and Jasper put a lot of effort into every inch of the place."

"They did an amazing job."

"Good afternoon," the woman behind the reception desk said.

Bessie smiled at Sandra Cook. Sandra had briefly worked at the little shop near Bessie's house, and Bessie had had an opportunity to get to know her well. She'd been instrumental in helping Sandra get a job at the Seaview, and she knew Sandra loved her job and that Jasper thought the world of the young woman.

"Good afternoon," Bessie replied.

"Mr. Coventry has put you in the penthouse today," Sandra told them. "And he had the pastry chef put together a collection of petit fours for you."

"How lovely," Bessie exclaimed.

"Jasper takes very good care of us," Andrew added.

"Mr. Coventry is happy that you've chosen to use our hotel for your meetings," Sandra replied.

"We're happy to be here," Bessie said.

"Especially in the penthouse with petit fours," Andrew added.

As they walked away from the desk, Bessie wondered if Jasper insisted that his staff call him Mr. Coventry or if Sandra preferred to use his title when talking with guests. She was still pondering the matter when they reached the top floor.

"Try one of everything," Hugh said as they walked into the penthouse conference room.

"It's a good thing we had a light lunch," Bessie said as she surveyed the delicious options on the table at the back of the room.

Andrew selected several things and then poured himself a cup of tea. Bessie followed suit. By the time she'd reached her chair, Doona and John had arrived. They were still filling plates when Harry and Charles walked into the room.

"Get what you want and have a seat," Andrew told them.

"I'm good," Harry said, taking a seat with his back to the wall.

Charles looked at the table and then poured himself a cup of coffee. As he took his seat, Andrew pulled a stack of envelopes out of his bag.

"Last month we were instrumental in helping to solve a particularly difficult set of murders," he said. "I think it's safe to say that we're now more in demand than ever. I have a huge stack of case summaries at home from police departments around the world."

"Does that mean you want us to start considering more than a single case each month?" Harry asked.

Andrew shook his head. "I did think about that, but it really isn't possible. You and Charles are both busy with your consultancy work. John and Hugh both work full-time for the constabulary here, and Doona is managing a holiday park in between cases. I don't think we have the time or the energy to increase our workload."

Harry nodded. "I wish we could, because catching killers is very satisfying, but I think you're right. I think we're doing as much as we can already."

"With that in mind, what I am doing is writing another book. This one is going to be about setting up and running a cold case unit. I would love to see hundreds of units being established around the world in the next decade," Andrew said.

"What a wonderful idea," Bessie said.

Charles nodded. "We have had unexpectedly brilliant success, but even if other units only manage the ten per cent that we were originally hoping for, they'll still be solving cases."

"Exactly," Andrew said. "I'd like each of you to write a chapter about yourself and your experiences in the unit. You won't be identified by name, but I want my readers to appreciate just how unusual this unit actually is."

Bessie frowned. "I don't think I can write an entire chapter," she said in a low voice.

"I'm going to give you each a rough outline of what I want in the chapters," Andrew said. "I hope I'm not asking too much of you."

He passed them each a sheet of paper. Bessie read down the extensive list of points he wanted them each to cover.

"I'm not sure this will all fit in a single chapter," she said with a laugh.

Everyone chuckled.

"Some of you may not want to address every point," Andrew said. "Only share what you are comfortable sharing. If at all possible, I'd like your chapters by the end of the year."

"I think I can manage that," Harry said.

"I'll get started today," Charles told him.

The others nodded. Bessie turned the sheet over and then looked expectantly at Andrew. While she would definitely write the chapter he wanted, she was more interested in this month's case than in anything else.

"I hope the case we're going to be considering this month will be somewhat easier than what we did last month," Andrew said. "This one seems as if it should have been solved. There are only four suspects."

"Is that absolutely certain?" Harry asked.

"As certain as it can be. Let me start at the beginning," Andrew replied.

Bessie had her notebook in front of her. She picked up her pen and looked at Andrew.

"As ever, I'm only going to give you a brief summary for today. You can read all the original statements tonight, and we'll meet again tomorrow to talk about your initial thoughts."

"And then you'll tell us where everyone is now, right?" Hugh asked.

Andrew nodded. "I'll give you updates on the suspects and copies of all of the statements they've given since the initial investigation."

"What part of the world are we in this time?" Harry asked.

"America, in the state of Pennsylvania. To be more specific, in the Allegheny National Forest."

"Campers?" Hugh asked.

"Exactly," Andrew replied. "A group of five men and women who decided to go camping for a weekend twelve years ago."

"Not exactly twelve years ago, I hope," Charles said. "I don't think camping in October is a good idea, is it?"

"People do it, but in this case it was late April. Apparently, everyone in the group was a keen camper, and they'd all been eagerly awaiting spring."

"Camping in tents or camping in nice cabins with hot and cold running water?" Doona asked.

Andrew smiled. "Tents. When I say they were keen campers, they parked several miles away from the site they intended to use, and they hiked into the forest with backpacks packed full of everything they thought they could possibly want for the weekend."

Bessie frowned. "I really don't understand how people find that enjoyable."

"It isn't my idea of a good time, either, but I'm told many people actually like it," Andrew replied.

"We did some camping when I was a child," Doona said. "It wasn't my idea of fun, either."

"Tell us about the five people," Harry said, seemingly annoyed with the off-topic conversation.

Bessie flushed and then wrote neat numbers from one to five down the page in her notebook.

Andrew cleared his throat. "In no particular order, the five were Douglas Moss, Rusty White, Mark Hogan, Patti Gardner, and Tina Fletcher. Patti is spelled with an 'I,' if that matters to anyone."

"And which one was the victim?" Harry asked.

"Let me start by telling you a bit about each of them," Andrew said. "Douglas Moss was twenty-five. Everyone called him Doug. He was single, and he worked as a bartender at a large hotel in downtown Pittsburgh."

Bessie made careful notes. Everything that Andrew was telling them would be in the case file, of course, but she found the files easier to follow if she had all of the basic information in one place before she started reading.

"Rusty White was twenty-six. He was also single, and he worked as a waiter at a restaurant across the street from the bar where Doug worked."

"Is that how they met?" Harry asked.

Andrew shook his head. "They'd known one another for years. They grew up in a Pittsburgh suburb and they went to the same college for a year."

"Only a year?" Doona asked.

"Doug dropped out after a year. Rusty lasted two years before he quit and got the job at the restaurant," Andrew explained.

"Who is next?" Charles asked.

"Mark Hogan was also twenty-five. He left his girlfriend behind in the city to go camping with his friends. His father owned the bar where Doug worked."

"Interesting," Harry said. "Did Mark work in the bar?"

"Mark worked for a large investment bank."

"So he had money," Harry suggested.

"He did," Andrew agreed. "At least, more money than any of the others."

"That's the men. What about the women?" Doona asked.

"Patti Gardner was twenty-three. She was seeing two different men, but neither relationship was serious. She was a waitress at the same restaurant as Rusty."

"And Tina?" Bessie asked.

"Tina Fletcher was twenty-nine."

"So, older than the others," Doona said.

"By a few years, yes," Andrew said. "She was divorced and apparently told everyone that she was done with men. Some of the others stated that she only came on the camping trip because she wanted to get closer to Mark, though."

"What did she do for a living?" Hugh asked.

"She didn't have a full-time job at the time of the camping trip, but she was occasionally filling in behind the bar where Doug worked when they were busy," Andrew replied.

"So the bar owner's son might have seemed to be a good catch," Harry said.

Andrew shrugged. "Mark already had a girlfriend. That's all my summary says, though. You'll have to read the file to find out more."

"So they all worked in the same part of Pittsburgh," John said. "Aside from Mark. How did he meet everyone?"

"Mark used to spend a lot of time in his father's bar," Andrew said. "Apparently he drank there most nights after work."

"Did they all live nearby?" Doona asked.

"Doug and Rusty both had flats not far from where they worked. They lived in different buildings, but the buildings were on the same street. They could walk from their flats to work in about ten minutes, or so I was told."

"And they'd known one another the longest," Harry said.

Andrew nodded. "Mark had a flat not all that far away, but it was several steps up in terms of quality. He was probably fifteen minutes away from his father's bar, but there was also a flat above the bar, and I'm told that Mark sometimes stayed there if he'd had too much to drink and didn't want to walk home."

"So he had a drinking problem," Charles said.

"See what you think after you've read the file," Andrew told him.

"What about Patti and Tina?" Bessie asked.

"Patti was sharing a flat with two other women around her age. They were farther away. Patti used to take a bus to the restaurant. Tina was staying with some friends in a small house in a residential area a few streets away from where Doug and Rusty lived. She told the police that it was only a temporary situation and that she'd be getting her own place soon."

"Could she walk to the bar from there?" Harry asked.

"She could, but apparently she usually took a bus."

"None of them had cars?" Hugh asked.

"Mark had a car, but when he went to the bar, he typically left it in the garage under the building where he had his flat."

"Okay, so now we know all about our little group of campers. What happened to them?" Harry asked.

CHAPTER 3

*A*ndrew took a sip of tea and then turned the page in his notebook. "Bars and restaurants are usually busiest on weekends," he said. "Everyone in the group agreed that it had been difficult for them all to get a weekend off together. Obviously, Mark didn't have that problem."

"Neither did Tina, really," Doona said. "Not if she was only working occasionally."

Andrew nodded. "The original plan had been for them to head to the Forest on Friday morning, but Mark had to work on Friday, so they decided that they'd leave right after Mark finished for the day. He had the car and was driving, of course."

"It must have been a big car to fit five people and all of their camping gear," Charles said.

"There are pictures of it in the file," Andrew told them. "It appears to have been plenty big enough."

"So they left on Friday afternoon," Harry said.

"Except they didn't," Andrew said. "That was the plan, but then Doug had to work. He was supposed to have the night off, but the man who was supposed to be taking his place fell ill. Mark's father, Michael, told Doug that he had to either come in or find someone to work the shift for him if he still wanted to have a job by Monday."

"And he couldn't find anyone?" Bessie asked.

"Apparently, he usually asked Tina to cover for him," Andrew said. "He rang Mark and told him what had happened, and after some debate, Mark agreed that they could leave on Saturday morning instead."

"When were they supposed to go back to Pittsburgh?" Doona wondered.

"The original plan was to spend Friday and Saturday night in the Forest and then drive back to Pittsburgh on Sunday afternoon, ideally as late as possible to still get back before dark. Because Doug had to work, the modified plan meant that they'd only be spending a single night in the Forest."

"How long was the drive?" Doona asked.

"It took them nearly three hours to get to the part of the Forest where they wanted to camp."

"It hardly seems worth it to go all that way for a single night," Hugh said.

"But apparently they were all keen to go, and they knew it would be a while before they could all get the same weekend off again," Andrew said.

"Had they all camped together before, then?" Bessie asked.

"Not in that exact group, but everyone in the group had been camping before and some people had camped with some of the others, if that makes sense."

"I think I know what you mean," Bessie said.

"How did the others usually get to the Forest, if only Mark had a car?" Hugh asked.

"Doug and Rusty used to borrow Rusty's sister's car," Andrew said. "She used to go with them sometimes, too. All of the details about their other trips are in the file. For now, let's focus on this trip."

Bessie made a note for herself to pay attention to who had camped with which of the others in the past.

"They left very early on Saturday morning," Andrew continued. "Mark drove down to the bar on Friday night and stayed there so that they could use the bar as their meeting point. They all agreed to be there by eight, but Tina was twenty minutes late."

"I'm surprised they didn't leave without her," Doona said.

"They would have if she'd been much later," Andrew said. "As it was, she arrived while they were packing up the car, so they still let her go along."

"I hope she wasn't the victim," Bessie said. "Although, if she wasn't, she probably deeply regrets getting there just in time."

"Unless she's the killer and she's pleased that she had a chance to kill the victim," Harry suggested.

"They left around half eight and drove most of the way before stopping for a short break," Andrew continued. "Then Mark drove them into the park until they reached the car park for the area where they wanted to camp."

"Who selected the area?" Harry asked.

"Doug and Rusty had camped in the Forest more than a dozen times the previous year. They were the ones who suggested the spot. Mark typically stayed at campsites within the park that had some amenities, but Doug and Rusty preferred a place they knew that wasn't a designated campsite."

"Did they need any special permission to camp there?" Bessie asked.

Andrew shook his head. "You can camp anywhere in most

parts of the Forest. The spot that Rusty and Doug preferred was in a small clearing. There was plenty of space for their three tents there. It was close to a spring that provided fresh water, and the clearing was surrounded by large trees that provided plenty of firewood."

"Where was the nearest café?" Doona asked.

Andrew chuckled. "Back at the entrance to the National Forest."

Doona sighed. "Not for me."

"How long did it take for them to hike from the car park to the campsite?" Harry asked.

"About an hour, but they stopped along the way to have lunch," Andrew told him. "When they reached the campsite, they set up their tents."

"You said there were three?" Harry asked.

"Yes, one for the women, one for Doug and Rusty, and a third for Mark," Andrew told him.

"And his was probably the nicest," Bessie guessed.

"Actually, they were all very nice tents," Andrew replied. "Mark supplied all three of them. Rusty and Doug usually just camped under a tarp in sleeping bags."

"What about bears?" Doona asked. "I mean, I wouldn't feel safe in a tent, either, but surely you're just asking to get eaten by a bear if you're just under a tarp?"

Andrew shrugged. "There are bears in the Allegheny National Forest. There are also snakes and mountain lions. I, personally, wouldn't camp there under any circumstances, but apparently Rusty and Doug weren't worried about the wildlife."

"But on this occasion they had tents," Harry said.

"Yes, they had tents supplied by Mark," Andrew said.

"Surely the women usually used tents rather than tarps," Doona said.

"Patti had her own tent, but it was only large enough for one person. When Mark offered to supply larger tents, she agreed that that would be a better option. Tina didn't own a tent, but usually stayed with friends who had tents she could share."

"Why did Mark offer to supply tents to everyone?" Hugh asked.

"According to him, he was just being kind," Andrew replied. "I gather he didn't want to sleep under a tarp and he didn't feel comfortable with being the only one in a nice tent."

"So they set up their tents, and then what?" Charles asked.

"Then they sat around the campfire and talked," Andrew replied. "They had some snacks and, after a while, they started drinking."

"Alcohol?" Harry checked.

"Yes, beer for the men and wine for the women."

"That must have been heavy for them to carry all that way," Hugh said.

"Each of them carried his or her own supply," Andrew said. "They took turns carrying the tents. I believe they had planned to bring more alcohol before they'd had to shorten the trip. As it was, each man had a six-pack of beer, and each woman brought a bottle of wine. When they first arrived at the campsite, they put everything in the stream to chill it. It was late April, but there was still snow on the peaks of the mountains, so the water was very cold."

"And then they all got drunk and started arguing," Harry guessed.

"Actually, no, they all got a little drunk and had some dinner and went to bed," Andrew told him. "All four of the witnesses said the same thing – that they'd had a nice evening together, laughing and talking about everything and nothing. The sun set not long after eight, and they all decided to head to bed about an hour later."

"Maybe they were all in on it together," Hugh suggested.

"That's one possibility that the police considered," Andrew said. "We'll have to see what we think after we've read the file."

"So Doug and Rusty went into one tent, the two women went into another, and Mark went into the third?" Bessie asked.

Andrew shook his head. "The tents were all supposed to be large enough for four people. When they headed to bed, Mark said that he'd rather not be alone, so he asked Rusty and Doug if he could share their tent. Obviously, they weren't going to say no, not when Mark was the one who'd supplied the tents in the first place."

"Does that mean that the third tent was left empty?" Hugh asked.

"It was. Mark told the women that one of them could use it if she wanted to, but they decided they'd be happier together. He made the same offer to Rusty and Doug but stipulated that he wanted to share with at least one of them. They decided they'd prefer to stay together, all three of them."

"Did Mark say why he didn't want to be alone?" Doona asked.

"This was his first time camping outside of the designated areas. He told the police in his interview that he found being all alone in the woods a bit spooky and that he would have preferred to have camped in one of the designated campsites instead."

"So they all went to bed and then something dreadful happened," Doona guessed.

"They all went to bed and, apparently, they all slept soundly. When they woke up the next morning, Doug was alone in the third tent. He'd been stabbed over a dozen times.

The knife was lying next to him. It was Doug's camping knife, and it had been wiped clean of fingerprints."

Bessie closed her eyes and slowly counted to ten as she felt a rush of sympathy for the poor young man who'd died years earlier.

"No one heard anything?" John asked. "Neither Mark nor Rusty noticed when Doug left the tent?"

"You'll have to read their statements to get the full answer, but, basically, no."

"So at some point in the night, Doug left their tent, went over to the other tent, went inside, and got murdered," Doona said.

Andrew nodded. "They'd strung twine between the trees all the way around their campsite and attached metal tins to the twine. It was supposed to be some sort of bear alarm. I don't know if it would have worked for that purpose, but it did seem to confirm that no strangers entered the campsite that night."

"How high was the twine? Could a person have just stepped over it?" Harry asked.

"In theory, yes, but that person would have had to have known it was there. There are pictures in the file, but the local police concluded that it was highly unlikely that anyone came into the site from outside."

"So that leaves us with four suspects," Harry said.

"Who found the body?" Bessie asked.

"Rusty. He was the first to wake up. He got up and restarted the campfire and put a pot of water on to make coffee. Then he stuck his head in the women's tent to say good morning. When he went back to his tent to say good morning to Doug and Mark, he realised that Doug wasn't there."

"He hadn't noticed when he woke up?" Hugh asked.

"Apparently, when he woke up, he was rather desperate to

relieve himself. He said he'd made his way out of the tent as quickly as he could without paying any attention to anything else."

"So when he realised that Doug was missing, what did he do?" Doona asked.

"He called his name a few times and then remembered the other tent. When he looked inside, he could immediately tell that something awful had happened."

"Were there lights in the tents?" Bessie asked.

"No, but they had clear panels across the top so that campers could lie inside and still see the forest around them. The panels gave Rusty enough light to see the body."

"Could he tell what had happened to him?" Doona asked.

"He told the police that he saw the body and lots of blood. He said his first thought was a bear attack or maybe a mountain lion, but there was no evidence that any wild animal had been anywhere near the campsite."

Bessie made a note. "What did he do next?"

"Swore a lot and then woke the others up. He told them what he'd seen. Mark laughed and said that Doug was probably just playing a trick on them. He went and looked in the tent and then came back and took charge."

"Why doesn't that surprise me?" Doona asked.

"Mark insisted that someone had to stay with the body while someone else went for help. Rusty was the one who knew the way back to the car park the best, so Mark told Rusty to head for the car park and ring for help from the pay phone there. Both of the women wanted to go with Rusty, but Mark said that one of them had to stay behind with him. He said he didn't want there to be any question that anyone had tampered with the body in any way."

"Smart, but it's also worrying that he was thinking so clearly about the upcoming investigation," Doona said.

"There had been a handful of bar fights in his father's bar

over the years," Andrew said. "And Mark had worked behind the bar while on breaks from university. He'd been questioned by the police on more than one occasion."

"Only as a witness?" Harry checked.

"Yes, only as a witness, but the experiences had given him some insight into how police investigations are conducted."

"He was right to be cautious," Charles said.

"He went and stood near the campfire while all of the others got dressed," Andrew continued. "Again, he didn't want to be accused of tampering with evidence. As soon as Rusty and Patti were ready, they headed back towards the car park. Tina and Mark sat around the campfire and waited for the police to arrive."

"What did they talk about while they waited?" Doona asked.

"It's all in their statements," Andrew told her. "But, apparently, they talked about the weather and bugs and how eager they were to get back to civilization."

"I can believe that," Doona said.

"How long did it take for the police to arrive?" Bessie asked.

"They walked back in with Rusty and Patti, arriving at the site about three hours after Rusty had found the body."

Bessie sighed. "That's a long time to talk about how badly they wanted out of there."

"You have pictures from the scene as well as a rough sketch of the location of the tents and the twine, um – fence isn't the right word, but I'm not certain what to call it."

"There probably wasn't a formal crime scene team, was there?" Harry asked.

Andrew shook his head. "The local police did their best, but I'm sure things were missed. All five of the campers had been inside the tent where the victim was found, though, so that complicated things."

"Why had they all been in the tent?" Doona asked.

"After all three tents had been erected, Mark gave them all a tour of them. They were all slightly different and he wanted everyone to see their options."

"Or he wanted to make sure that everyone left fingerprints in the tent where he was planning to leave the body," Hugh suggested.

Andrew shrugged. "Also possible."

"Anything else?" Harry asked.

Andrew checked his notes. "The police took initial statements at the campsite and follow-up statements the next day in Pittsburgh. You have both of those pairs statements in your file. All four of the campers have been interviewed multiple times since. I'll give you those statements tomorrow, after I give you a brief update on everyone."

"Did Mark drive everyone back to Pittsburgh? Did they pack up the other two tents and take them with them?" Hugh asked.

"The police took everything at the campsite, including the rubbish, as evidence. Nolan, the officer in charge of the investigation, noted that the police later offered to give the other two tents back to Mark, but he told them that he didn't want them. They were eventually sent to a police auction."

"How much later?" Charles asked.

Andrew checked his notes again. "He didn't say. It's probably in the file. Regardless, Mark did drive everyone back to Pittsburgh once the police gave them permission to leave. As I said, they were all interviewed again the next day."

"And that's all we're going to get today, isn't it?" Charles asked.

Andrew nodded. "I think that's enough for now. I feel as if I've given you more than I normally do, but Nolan provided an excellent summary – one that caught my interest right away."

"I'll see you all tomorrow, then," Harry said as he got to his feet.

Andrew flipped through the envelopes in front of him and found the one with Harry's name on it. He handed it to Harry as Charles got up.

"Thanks," Harry said. He was out the door before Andrew had found Charles's envelope.

"Thanks," Charles echoed a moment later.

As the door shut behind Charles, Hugh grinned. "Do you think I can take a few things for later?" he asked, nodding towards the table at the back of the room.

"Jasper left boxes," Bessie said, gesturing towards the small stack under the table.

"So he did," Hugh said happily.

Andrew passed out the rest of the envelopes, and then everyone put a few treats into boxes to take home. Hugh filled two for himself.

"This one is for me and Aalish," he said. "The second one is all for Grace. She's working hard, making a baby. She deserves lots of extra treats."

"Give her a hug from me," Bessie said. "And remind her that she's welcome to visit me if she wants a cuppa and a sympathetic ear."

Hugh nodded. "I'm sure she'd love that, but Aalish is getting into absolutely everything right now. I'm not sure your cottage would survive half an hour with my daughter."

John grinned. "I don't miss those days, although teenagers bring their own challenges."

"Thomas is across now, isn't he?" Andrew asked.

"He is, and I miss him, but so far he seems to love university," John replied. "Amy is miserable, though."

"She adores her older brother," Doona said. "Now that he's gone, she feels rather alone in the world."

"She's also welcome to visit any time," Bessie said.

Doona nodded. "An afternoon with Aunt Bessie might be exactly what she needs."

The group walked out to the lifts together. Back in the lobby, Jasper was busy at reception, dealing with a short queue of people. Bessie just waved as they all walked out of the hotel together.

"Back to Laxey?" Andrew asked as they got into his hire car.

"Yes, please. I'm eager to get started on the case."

"It does seem as if it should have been solved. There were only four suspects."

"Unless the police were wrong, and someone came into the campsite from elsewhere."

"That's a possibility, of course, but how did that someone get Doug into the other tent?"

Bessie sighed. "Maybe Doug wanted his own space. Maybe he went over to the other tent and that caught the attention of some random person who was walking past. Maybe that random person decided it would be a good idea to kill Doug. Or maybe Doug saw the person doing something illegal or immoral and the person killed Doug to get rid of the witness."

"See how you feel after you read the file and study the pictures of the site," Andrew suggested.

A few minutes later, Andrew parked near Bessie's cottage.

"I'll just walk through your cottage," he said. "Then I'll leave you to get to work."

Bessie swallowed a sigh. She appreciated his concern, especially since her cottage had been broken into during a murder investigation years earlier, but she was also eager to get to work.

"Should we try making plans again?" Andrew asked after he'd come back from checking the first floor.

"Dinner?"

"I'll come over at six. We can go somewhere in Laxey if you're in a hurry to get back to the case file."

"Will Helen be joining us?"

"Probably, but maybe we can have a short conversation about the case after dinner."

Bessie grinned. He knew exactly why she'd asked. "Perfect. I'll see you and Helen at six."

CHAPTER 4

Bessie filled the kettle and switched it on. As she put her envelope on the table, she noticed the light flashing on her answering machine.

"Bessie, it's Breesha. I have some information for you. Ring me back when you have a minute."

Bessie made her tea and then sat down with her envelope and her notebook. Before she started work, though, she picked up the telephone and rang Breesha.

"Ah, Bessie, I wasn't certain you'd get back to me today."

"I didn't expect to hear from you for ages."

Breesha chuckled. "Once you'd put the idea in my head, I couldn't think of anything I wanted to do more than drive up to Jurby and see what I could find."

"I hope Doncan didn't mind."

"He knows better than to complain, even if he does mind," she laughed.

"Did you actually manage to find something?"

"Of course. We keep meticulous records, you know."

"Of course, I never doubted you."

"You purchased your cottage from Ewan and Margaret Christian," Breesha told her.

"All common Manx names, of course."

"Yes, of course."

"I have a vague recollection of meeting them when I first visited the cottage," Bessie said, trying to think back over the decades. "If I'm correct, then Ewan was very much alive at the time."

"He and Margaret both signed all of the paperwork pertaining to the sale."

"I'm going to assume that it wasn't named Widow's Cottage by them, then."

"Probably not."

"So we need to go back farther in the records."

"What can I do to help?"

Bessie chuckled. "You're curious now, too, aren't you?"

"I am. I never gave the name of your cottage any thought, and now I can't stop thinking about it. We have an assistant who researches the sales history of properties before our clients purchase them. Do you want me to see what he can find?"

"Let me see what I can do myself first. It will probably have to wait a fortnight or so, but once we wrap up this month's cold case meetings, I'll have time to do some research in the Manx Museum Library. I need to work backwards and try to find out when the cottage was given its name."

"And the library should have that information, somewhere."

"Exactly, it's just a matter of finding it. Thank you for your help," Bessie said. "I'll let you know if I find out anything further."

"Please do, and don't hesitate to ask for more help if you need it."

Bessie put the phone down and took a sip of tea. The afternoon was getting away from her, but she couldn't resist picking up the phone again. She expected that she'd have to leave a message for Marjorie, but the woman answered.

"Hello?"

"Marjorie, hello. It's Bessie Cubbon."

"Ah, Bessie, I was going to ring you later."

"Were you?"

"I've been through Woods' Atlas. The land where your cottage sits was part of a much larger parcel that was owned by a George Christian. The Atlas only identifies who owns the land, of course. It doesn't show what buildings were on the land."

"And he may or may not have been related to the couple from whom I bought the cottage."

"Did you get the name of the previous owner, then?"

"Yes, I bought the cottage from Ewan and Margaret Christian."

"I can do some digging and see what I can find in the parish registers about them."

"I thought I'd do that myself, but it might have to wait for a fortnight."

"I probably wouldn't be able to get to it for at least a month, so I'll leave it with you," Marjorie said with a laugh. "I've left instructions for one of my assistants to search the catalogues for references to your cottage in the archives. I can't promise we'll find anything, but we might. Of course, there could be items in there that haven't been indexed as well."

"Of course. I appreciate all of your help."

"You know I'm happy to do it. I'm quite curious now, actually, about how the cottage got its name."

"I'll let you know if I find anything."

"I'll look forward to seeing you in the library in a fortnight."

"Thank you."

As Bessie put the phone down, she frowned. A fortnight seemed like a very long time, really. Having lived in the cottage for more years than she wanted to admit, she was suddenly eager to find out as much as she could about its previous owners.

"Not all of them, just the ones who gave it its name," she muttered as she carefully opened her envelope.

When Andrew knocked on her door a few hours later, Bessie was happy to put the paperwork away and take a break.

"Ready for dinner?" Andrew asked.

"More than. The file has my head spinning."

Andrew raised an eyebrow. "We can have a quick conversation now if that would help. Helen should be here soon, though."

"No, let's leave it for after dinner. I'd rather not think about the case at all for an hour or two."

"I can understand that."

Bessie went up to her room to comb her short grey hair. She added some lipstick to her lips and then headed back down the stairs. Helen was standing with her father in the kitchen when Bessie arrived.

"How are you?" Bessie asked as she pulled on her shoes.

"Grumpy," Helen replied, with a small laugh that sounded forced. "Work was incredibly stressful today."

"I'm sorry to hear that," Bessie said.

"I love my job, but there are days when I think I'd be happier doing just about anything else."

"We all have those days," Andrew told her.

Bessie nodded. "The cold case unit does a lot of good, and

I'm grateful that I get to be a part of it, but reading case files can be terribly upsetting and difficult."

Helen made a face. "I can't imagine. As much as I complain, I'd much rather do what I do than read case files about brutal murders."

"And, on that note, let's go and have a nice quiet dinner," Andrew suggested.

"Where are we going?" Helen asked as they all got into the car.

"What about the Italian place here in Laxey?" Andrew asked. "I know we eat there every time we come to the island, but the food is excellent."

"I'll never complain about eating there," Bessie said.

"Italian sounds good to me," Helen agreed.

They had a delicious meal, including pudding, and then Andrew drove them back to Laxey Beach.

"And now I shall go and soak in a hot bath with a good book and forget all about the day," Helen said. "Don't be too late," she told her father. "You're still tired from travelling."

Andrew nodded. "Bessie and I will just have a quick chat."

Helen looked at Bessie. "Send him home soon," she said.

"I will," Bessie promised.

Inside Treoghe Bwaane, Andrew did a quick check of the cottage while Bessie put the kettle on. When he came back from checking the first floor, Bessie waved him into a chair.

"I'll just make us some tea and then we can talk," she said.

"How far did you get in the case file?"

"I've read all the initial statements and the ones from the next day. I will admit that I read them very quickly, though. I plan to go back through them all again before our meeting tomorrow."

"So what did you think of the suspects?"

Bessie thought for a minute. "I didn't really care for any of them. As always, I'm frustrated because I want to meet them and talk to them in person. Of course, they're all twelve years older now. They're probably very different people."

"Indeed. I haven't looked at the updates yet, but I'm very curious to find out where everyone is now."

Bessie made the tea and then put their cups on the table. "I ate too much at dinner to want any biscuits," she told Andrew. "I'm happy to put some out for you, though, if you want some."

He shook his head. "I'm stuffed. I shouldn't have had the tiramisu, but it sounded too good to pass up."

"I hope you enjoyed it."

"It was wonderful. Not the best I've ever had, but very close."

"That's good to hear."

Andrew took a sip of tea and then smiled at Bessie. "Where do you want to start?"

"We could start with Mark. I disliked him the most."

Andrew chuckled. "I think we'll all feel that way. He came across in his interviews as arrogant and not at all concerned about the death of his friend."

"Were they friends, though? Mark certainly doesn't talk about Doug with any sort of affection. I felt as if Doug and the others were the people that Mark spent time with when he felt like spending time with some less fortunate people, if you know what I mean."

"I do know what you mean. Mark talked a lot about how little time he typically spent with Doug and the others."

"The others mostly agreed," Bessie said. "Patti said she was surprised when she found out that he was going on the camping trip with them."

"Let's talk about how the trip was arranged in the first place."

"There was something odd there. Rusty said that it was

Mark's idea to take a group to the Forest as soon as the weather was good enough."

"But Patti said that Doug was the one who suggested it to her and that once she'd agreed, he'd said he'd try to persuade Rusty and some others to join them."

"I couldn't work out where Tina fit into all of that, either," Bessie said.

"She said she'd heard about the trip and decided she wanted to go along."

"Patti suggested that Tina only wanted to go because she'd heard that Mark was going to be there, but Tina said she didn't know who was involved, just that there was going to be a group going camping that weekend."

"I'm not certain I believed her," Andrew said.

"I'm not either. Rusty and Patti both said that Tina was only there because of Mark."

"No one was clear on when the trip was first discussed."

"Rusty said they'd all been talking all winter long about going away, but none of them wanted to try camping in the snow." Bessie stared at him. "Do people actually camp in the snow?"

"I believe so."

"How unpleasant."

"I suppose if you dug out a snowdrift you could make yourself a quite snug little shelter."

"Or you could stay home in the nice warm house you already have and watch the snow falling outside the window."

Andrew laughed. "Yes, okay, I do prefer your idea."

Bessie sighed. "I know none of them realised at the time how important it was going to be, but I can't help but feel that we'd be a lot closer to finding the killer if we knew how the weekend away was planned."

"It's possible, of course, that Doug was behind a lot of the planning."

"It sounded very much like something that was discussed over drinks in the bar throughout the winter. Then, when the weather finally improved, they started making firm plans."

"According to Patti, including Doug there were eight people who regularly drank in the bar at least a few nights a week. She said she used to go over after her shift in the restaurant whenever she wasn't working until closing."

"Doug was nearly always there, of course. Everyone agreed that he rarely drank much until towards the end of the evening. Then he might let someone buy him a drink or two."

"Rusty said he went over every night, even if he did have to work until closing. The restaurant stopped serving at midnight, but the bar was open until two, so he could always get at least one drink after they'd chased the last customers out of the restaurant."

"Tina said she only drank there once in a while, but everyone else said they saw her there at least once a week, sometimes more often."

"And then there's Mark," Andrew said with a sigh.

"Patti included him in the group, but I don't think he would have wanted to be considered a part of it."

"He said he spent time there mostly to keep an eye on things on his father's behalf."

"It's hard to imagine he did that very well after his fifth or sixth drink," Bessie said dryly.

"Yes, everyone else said that Mark used to drink quite a lot when he was there."

"While Mark said he usually sipped one or two drinks all night."

"He did admit that he often slept in the flat above the bar, but he told Nolan that he knew better than to drive after drinking even a single drink."

"Which is fair enough, I suppose," Bessie said.

"Should we talk about the other three people whom Patti considered part of their group?"

"I don't see much point. None of them were on the camping trip, and they all had alibis for the night of the murder."

Andrew nodded. "I found it interesting that they were all at a party together."

"I did wonder if any of the others had been invited to that party. I don't think they were asked about it when they were questioned."

"I don't think they were. Nolan probably didn't think it mattered."

"And it probably doesn't. I'm just trying to get a better understanding of the dynamics within the group. There were eight people who regularly spent time together in a bar. One weekend, five of them went camping while the other three went to a party. Were the three who went to the party invited on the camping trip? And were the five on the camping trip invited to the party?"

"I can have Nolan ask our four suspects those questions, but I'm not certain he'll want to try to track down the other three friends to ask them about the party."

"Maybe we can come up with more questions for those three."

"We don't know exactly how the camping trip was arranged. I can ask Nolan to try to pin that down, but it's been twelve years. I doubt anyone will remember more now than they did when they were questioned originally."

"And if they do remember more, I'd wonder why."

"There is that. You said you didn't care for Mark. What about the others?"

"I liked Rusty better, which isn't saying much. He'd dropped out of college because he didn't know what he wanted to do with his life, but, years later, he still hadn't made any decisions. He insisted that he didn't intend to be a waiter forever, but he said he hadn't really thought about what he might want to do instead."

"He seemed happy enough with his life, though. He made decent money at the restaurant, and he had friends to spend time with when he wasn't working."

"The restaurant manager said he was good at his job. She said he remembered their regular customers and worked hard."

"Anything else about Rusty?"

"I thought he seemed a bit sweet on Patti, but I may be reading too much into some of his remarks."

"I thought he came across as somewhat protective of her, which made sense, because she seemed somewhat naïve."

Bessie nodded. "She'd been working as a waitress since she'd graduated from high school at nineteen, working her way from a small diner to a larger coffee shop to a small restaurant before she got the job at the larger and fancier restaurant where she was working at the time of the murder."

"She'd moved flats as often as she'd moved jobs, too. She'd been in the flat she was sharing with two other women for just a few months."

"She said she'd moved because that flat was closer to work. For the first three months she'd worked there, she'd needed to take two different buses to get to work."

"And she was seeing two different men, which makes her sound less innocent than she seemed."

"She did say that neither relationship was anything serious. One of the men lived in her building, and from what she said, they occasionally grabbed coffee together if they saw each other in the corridor, but that was the extent of the relationship."

"And the other man was the manager of the restaurant where she had formerly worked," Andrew said. "She said the restaurant had rules about not getting involved with work colleagues, but they'd bumped into each other about a month before the murder and he'd asked her to have dinner with him."

"From what she said, they'd only gone out a handful of times."

"Yes, and she didn't sound all that interested in him."

"Neither of them is really relevant to the investigation, since they were both at home in Pittsburgh on the night of the murder," Bessie said. "Which means the only person we haven't discussed is Tina."

"Who was bitter about her divorce, angry that she couldn't find a job, and seemingly furious that her weekend with Mark had been interrupted."

"She did come across as a very unhappy person. From what she said about her ex-husband, I can see why she was bitter about her divorce, but, unfortunately, he's not a suspect, either."

"He was at home with his new girlfriend and several of her friends, celebrating."

"Because the new girlfriend was pregnant. Tina found out just a day or two before the trip, and that made her even more bitter, because she'd wanted children and her ex had always insisted that he didn't."

"She seemed more angry than sad about Doug's death."

"Because she'd been hoping to get close to Mark on the weekend away, or so everyone seemed to think."

Andrew nodded. "Even Mark seemed to think that, which seemed to have amused him."

"I hope he treated Tina more kindly in person than he did when talking about her in his interview."

"He was rather dismissive of her."

"She was very pretty."

"She was, and she was blonde, which was what everyone said Mark preferred."

"Of course, Mark already had a girlfriend. I'd love to know more about Mindy, but only because I'm nosy. She was in Florida the night of the murder."

"She and Mark didn't seem to spend much time together."

Bessie nodded. "Nolan had someone take her statement from Florida, where she was holidaying with her parents. She told the local police that she and Mark had been seeing one another for about a year, but that it wasn't anything serious. I got the impression that she was only hanging on to him while she was waiting for someone better to come along."

Andrew laughed. "That's rather terrible, but I know exactly what you mean, and I think you're right."

Before Bessie could speak again, someone knocked on the door.

"Who could that be?" Andrew asked.

"Helen," Bessie guessed.

Andrew made a face and then walked to the door.

"I am an adult," he told his daughter.

Helen laughed. "I know you are, but it's getting late, and you're exhausted. Besides, Matt just rang. He's had some news about the divorce and he wants your advice."

"You'd better go," Bessie said. "We were just about finished, anyway, and we have an entire fortnight to talk about the case."

Andrew gave her a hug and then followed Helen out of the cottage. Bessie watched them walk back to their holiday cottage, and then she slowly shut the door. After checking that it was securely locked, she headed up to bed.

CHAPTER 5

"Good morning," Helen called as Bessie stepped out of her cottage the next morning.

"Good morning," Bessie replied. "How are you this morning?"

"I slept well. After a nice walk, I think I'll be ready for whatever work throws at me today."

They fell into step together, walking along the water's edge.

"Perhaps today will be a better day."

"I certainly hope so. I am sorry that I interrupted last night."

"You shouldn't be. You were only doing what you thought was best for your father, who isn't very good at looking after himself."

Helen laughed. "He's quite dreadful at it, really. I get incredibly frustrated with him sometimes."

"I hope the news that Matt received was good news."

"It was. It's starting to look as if the divorce will go through soon. His wife seems to have decided to stop fighting."

"That's good to hear."

"I believe she finally realised that every penny Matt has to give to his solicitors to fight back means one less penny she can try to convince the courts that she deserves."

"I suspect Matt will just be happy to have it all finished."

"Indeed. He told me last night that he'd give her his very last pound if she'd just go away."

"I hope it doesn't come to that."

"It won't. Dad is paying for Matt's solicitors, and they're some of the best in the business. That's probably another reason why his ex is suddenly so eager to settle everything. She should have agreed to Matt's first offer two years ago. She would have done a lot better than she will now."

"Ready to turn around?" Bessie asked as they reached the stairs to Thie yn Traie.

"Tell me again about the people who own that giant mansion up there," Helen said, nodding towards the house perched on the cliff above them.

Bessie looked up and smiled. From the beach, all that was visible was the huge wall of windows that marked the end of the house's great room.

"I should take you there one day," she said. "The owners are friends of mine. Once you climb the stairs, you can see all of the house's many wings."

"How many?"

Bessie thought for a minute. "Too many," she said with a laugh. "I'm not entirely certain, though. I don't believe I've seen the entire house, although I've been around quite a lot of it."

"Imagine having entire wings in your home."

"Imagine having to clean entire wings," Bessie countered.

Helen laughed. "Why do I doubt that your friends are cleaning their own house?"

"They aren't, of course. They have staff, but I can't imagine that, either."

"It would be odd."

Bessie shook her head. "But you asked about the owners. The original owners built the house as a summer home."

Helen stared at her for a moment. "They built a huge house with multiple wings as a summer home?"

Bessie told her the name of the man who'd built the property.

"I know the name, and I can imagine them having houses that size all over the world, really."

"They used to come over every summer for a few months, but after a family tragedy on the island, they decided to sell the house."

Helen snapped her fingers. "That's why the name is so familiar. Didn't one of their sons murder the other?"

Bessie frowned. "Yes, and I found the body."

Helen pulled her into a quick hug. "I am sorry."

"It was pretty awful. I'd never seen a dead body outside of a funeral home before that."

"So they decided to sell the house," Helen said, clearly eager to move the conversation along.

"Yes, and my friends George and Mary Quayle bought it."

"I believe I've met George. My father introduced us once when we were in Douglas. If I'm thinking of the right man, he's large and loud and everything he says sounds as if he's trying to sell you something."

Bessie grinned. "That's George."

"I can't imagine what his wife is like."

"Mary is very quiet and shy. While George loves nothing more than a party, Mary prefers to be at home with her children and grandchildren."

"Proof, I suppose, that opposites attract."

"I suppose so."

"How many children do they have?"

"Three, two boys and a girl. The boys, who are men, of course, both work with George now. Their daughter, Elizabeth, has a party planning business."

"I remember you talking about her before. You said her business is very successful, didn't you?"

"It was very successful when she started it. Then she took an extended holiday with her parents. She's been struggling to rebuild it ever since."

"There was a man involved," Helen said.

Bessie sighed. "Andy Caine. He's a brilliant chef. He and Elizabeth started working together once he returned to the island after he'd completed culinary school. They also had a personal relationship."

"Which wasn't helped when Elizabeth went away."

"They ended their relationship before she left. Andy then started seeing someone else, who also had a party planning business."

"Is the island big enough to support two such businesses?"

"I don't know. We may find out some day, but the other woman is no longer here. It turned out that she'd filled Andy's head with a number of incredibly hurtful lies about Elizabeth. When Andy found out that she was lying, she left the island."

"I don't suppose he and Elizabeth got back together and lived happily ever after?"

"Not yet, but I live in hope," Bessie said.

Helen laughed. "Knowing you, you're doing more than just hoping."

"I'm doing everything I can to support them both in their personal and professional lives. Andy is in the process of purchasing the house in Lonan that you toured with your father and me some months ago."

"The huge, gorgeous one? Ah, and that's the Andy you

were talking about? He's very handsome and he seemed quite smart, if a bit indecisive."

Bessie laughed. "He's all of those things. He probably would never have made an offer on the house if Elizabeth hadn't said she wanted it."

"Was she going to buy it just to get back at him?"

"Quite the opposite. She simply pretended to be interested in order to force his hand. She knew he wanted it, but that he'd never make the decision if he didn't have to make it."

"That was kind of her."

"She's still in love with him, of course. And he's still in love with her, but neither of them will admit that to themselves or anyone else."

Helen sighed. "Life and love can be far too complicated sometimes."

"Indeed."

They'd reached Helen's cottage. She stopped and smiled at Bessie. "Thank you for the walk and the story. I'll probably forget everything you said and ask about the mansion's owners again every month."

"You've no reason to remember anything about them, really."

"What's the name of the mansion?"

"Thie yn Traie. It means 'Beach House' in Manx."

"If I ever bought a house here, I'd want to give it a Manx name."

"Are you considering buying a house here?"

Helen shrugged. "My father and I have been talking about buying something together. It would make sense for him to have a place here, since he's here so regularly. I just love the idea of owning half of a holiday home. Having a second home seems like something only the very wealthy do, really."

"If I can do anything to help, please let me know."

"Oh, we will."

Bessie continued the rest of the way to her cottage and went inside. Then she curled up with the case file and read until her stomach was growling too loudly to be ignored. As she walked into the kitchen, someone knocked on her door.

"I slept incredibly late," Andrew said. "And now I'm starving."

"I can make sandwiches, or we can go out somewhere."

"Let's head to the Seaview. We can have lunch there today to make up for not going yesterday."

"Give me ten minutes to get ready."

"I'll be waiting by my car."

Fifteen minutes later, they were on their way to Ramsey.

"I didn't just sleep late," Andrew said as he drove. "Once I woke up, I went back through the case file."

"And did you find anything interesting?"

He sighed. "I wish. I read the accounts of the evening over and over again, wishing that one of them had seen or heard something."

"One of them did."

Andrew chuckled. "Yes, of course. The murderer saw and heard everything, but I find it odd that the others slept through it all."

"Is it possible that they were doing more than just drinking?"

"You're suggesting that they were taking drugs."

"I'm just wondering if it's possible."

"I thought the same thing. I'm going to ask Nolan about it."

"I spent some time on those sections of the statements today, too. If they weren't taking drugs, is it possible that the killer added something to their food or drinks to make sure that they all slept soundly?"

"Another possibility. Every one of them commented on

sleeping very well, but they all seemed to credit the mountain air for their deep sleep."

"And that may be correct, but I find it hard to believe that Doug got up and left the tent and neither Mark nor Rusty noticed."

"Maybe we should tape out the dimensions of the tent on the floor and then see just how close together the men were sleeping."

"That isn't a bad idea. Mark said that Doug was the closest to the tent flap, and that he'd requested that space because he said he'd probably need to get up to, um, relieve himself during the night. He also said that, if he had noticed Doug moving around, he would have just assumed that he was going out for that reason and ignored him."

"And that it could have happened, but if it did, he didn't remember it."

Bessie sighed. "Which is one of the reasons why I thought he might not be the killer. Surely, if he were the killer, he'd say that he heard Doug leave during the night but that he rolled over and went back to sleep."

"Maybe, or maybe he's decided it's best to just pretend to know nothing."

Andrew pulled into the hotel's car park. "Perhaps before we go to lunch we should find out what we're going to have in the conference room today."

Bessie laughed. "That's a good idea. I'd hate to eat too much lunch if we have something wonderful."

"It's just biscuits today," Sandra told them when they asked at reception. "I am sorry, but we have two weddings this weekend. The chef and the pastry chef are both busy getting things ready for those."

"You've no need to be sorry," Bessie assured her. "We're only paying for biscuits, after all."

Sandra laughed. "You do have some very fancy biscuits,"

she said, leaning over the counter and speaking in a low voice. "The pastry chef was asked to make two hundred heart-shaped biscuits with the initials of the bride and groom on them. He'd already decorated the first hundred when someone noticed that he was putting the wrong initials on them."

"Oh, dear. Had he mixed up the two weddings?"

"If only it were that simple. Jasper would have been happy to give the other couple a hundred fancy biscuits as a special wedding gift from the hotel, but the pastry chef put D and S on every biscuit. That's the bride from one wedding and the groom from the other."

Bessie laughed. "Perhaps he knows something that we do not," she said.

Sandra frowned. "Oh, I hope not. The last thing we need is for a fight to break out during the two parties."

"Are they at the same time on the same day?" Andrew asked.

"They're both on Saturday. One starts a few hours after the other, though, and as far as I know, the couples don't know one another."

"I'm sure it was a simple mistake on the part of the pastry chef."

"Can't you just redecorate them?" Andrew asked.

Sandra shook her head. "The pastry chef tried, but Jasper was appalled at the result. I thought they still looked lovely, but Jasper could tell that they'd been scraped and redecorated, and he insisted that they all needed to be redone."

"You don't maintain your reputation as the island's premier wedding event space if you cut corners," Jasper said as he emerged from the door behind Sandra. "Besides, I thought my favourite cold case unit would appreciate some very fancy biscuits."

"We will, of course," Bessie said.

"And now, if you've come for lunch, let me walk you to the dining room. While we walk, I'll tell you about today's lunch specials."

Because Jasper showed them to seats in the dining room, their waiter was very attentive. Bessie enjoyed her chicken casserole and only reluctantly passed on pudding.

"We do have biscuits in the conference room," Andrew reminded her as they got up to leave the room.

"Yes, I know, and I'm looking forward to trying the poor unwanted wedding ones."

When they walked into the penthouse conference room, Bessie immediately headed to the back of the room to inspect the biscuits.

"We have several options, but I'm most eager to try these heart-shaped ones," Bessie said, putting three on a plate.

"They look very good."

"The lettering is very beautifully done."

"And they taste delicious," Andrew said after a bite.

Bessie grinned and tried one herself. "They are very good," she agreed.

She added an extra one to her plate and then poured herself some tea. As she settled into her seat, John, Doona, and Hugh all arrived at once. They were laughing over the biscuit story when Harry and Charles arrived. Once everyone was seated, Andrew cleared his throat.

"I hope you've all had time to read through the initial statements," he said.

A few people nodded.

"I'm dying to know where everyone is now," Doona said.

"Before we get to that, I'd like to talk about what you all thought of the suspects based on their statements right after the murder," Andrew said.

"I didn't like any of them," Doona said. "But Mark was the worst. He's at the top of my list."

"Mine, too," Hugh said. "The other three are tied for second place on my list."

Doona frowned. "I'd put Rusty next, under Mark, then Tina, and then Patti."

Harry nodded. "My list is the same. Mark, Rusty, Tina, and then Patti."

"I'd actually go Mark, Tina, Rusty, Patti," Charles said. "Tina was angry at the world. Maybe she took that out on Doug."

"My list goes, Mark, Rusty, Tina, and then Patti," John said. "But there isn't a lot separating any of them. I'm hoping that when we hear where they all are now, it might help."

"Bessie, what about your list?" Andrew asked.

She shrugged. "Mark is first, then I'd put Tina and Rusty on the same line, with Patti last. Except now that we've all put her last, I'm starting to suspect her more."

Everyone chuckled.

"I know what you mean," Charles said. "She seemed quite naïve, but maybe it was all an act."

"Where is everyone on your list?" Bessie asked Andrew.

"Mark is at the top. I'd put Rusty next, but Tina isn't far behind. Patti is last on my list, too," he replied.

"I couldn't work out how one of the women could have sneaked out of her tent and managed to get Doug out of his," Doona said.

"They either arranged it in advance, or maybe she was lying in her tent watching for him," Andrew suggested. "Doug did say that he knew he'd have to get up at least once in the night."

"Why didn't any of the others?" Doona asked. "Even at twenty-something, if I'd drunk an entire bottle of wine, I'd have needed to get up and go behind a rock at least once in the night."

"That's a good point," Andrew said. "Bessie and I were

discussing the possibility that they weren't just drinking, though."

"I can't imagine being so out of it that I could ignore nature calling," Doona said.

"Rusty did say that he got up because he needed to go," Hugh said. "And the others all said that they took care of that first thing, too."

"I was wondering if the killer slipped sleeping tablets into everyone's food," Doona said. "That would explain why they all slept so well."

Andrew nodded. "Bessie had the same idea."

"I suppose it's far too late now to find out anything conclusive," Hugh said.

Andrew nodded. "They would have had to run tests on samples from the suspects immediately."

"There's nothing in the file to suggest that the police ever considered that possibility," John said.

"I'll talk to Nolan. It's possible that they considered it but never actually made a note of it in the file. It's also possible that they considered it but decided that it wasn't possible."

"It seems to be the only explanation for how someone was able to commit a murder practically under everyone's noses," Hugh said.

"They were drunk," Doona said.

"But were they?" Harry asked. "They all admitted that they drank regularly. It's possible that six beers or a bottle of wine in an evening wasn't enough to make them drunk."

"They all might have just been mildly intoxicated," Charles said.

"Just drunk enough to sleep through a murder," Bessie murmured.

"Patti was very upset about that," Doona said. "At one point, she seemed to blame herself for the murder."

John nodded. "She was the most upset of anyone, both about the murder and about the victim."

"Yeah, I did wonder about Doug. These were his friends, but none of them seemed all that broken up about his death," Doona said.

"Bessie wondered about the party back in Pittsburgh that the five of them were missing," Andrew said.

Doona nodded. "I wondered about that, too. Patti said there were eight in their group, but only five of them went camping that night. The other three were at a party. Why?"

"I can't see that it matters," Harry said. "The party gave the other three friends unbreakable alibis, but, otherwise, it's irrelevant to the murder."

"But it's relevant to their lives," Bessie said. "Or it might be. I want to know more because I want to understand more about how the various friendships worked. Were those other three friends more upset than the four suspects when they found out that Doug was dead? Did they care more about him than the people with whom he'd gone camping?"

Harry shrugged. "None of them killed the man. That's what we're investigating."

"I'll see if Nolan can find out more," Andrew said. "But that's going to be a lower priority than our other questions, assuming we have some."

A few people exchanged glances.

"Aside from the issue of whether they were taking drugs or not that night, either voluntarily or involuntarily, I think I'd prefer to read the updates before we send questions back to Nolan," Harry said.

Andrew nodded. "That's fine. I'm going to send him a message tonight with some of our preliminary thoughts, but I don't think he should go back and question anyone again until after our next meeting."

"We aren't meeting tomorrow, are we?" Hugh asked.

"No, we're not. I want you to have plenty of time to read through the updates and then come up with questions for Nolan."

I wonder if I'd have time for a trip to the archives, Bessie thought.

"I hope you're going to give us the updates now, then," Harry said.

Andrew nodded. "For today, I'll just tell where everyone is now."

Bessie picked up her pen, eager to discover what had happened to the four young men and women who'd been camping that night.

CHAPTER 6

"Let's start with Mark," Andrew said. "I would imagine he's the one you are all most interested in hearing about. Does anyone want to speculate on where he is now?"

"Still working for a bank. Still arrogant and dreadful," Doona guessed.

"Or maybe he owns the bar now," Hugh said. "Maybe his father decided to retire and gave the bar to Mark."

"I suspect he's married with a few children, but he cheats regularly," Doona added. "His wife probably knows and doesn't care."

Andrew grinned. "You really didn't care for the man, did you?"

She shook her head. "He definitely seemed like the type to cheat."

Andrew looked at his notes. "Mark is not married, but he does have a girlfriend. They've been together for a year or so, but Mark told Nolan that it isn't serious."

"Surprise, surprise," Doona muttered.

"And Hugh was correct. Mark now owns the bar. His

father passed away just a couple of years after the murder. He left the bar to Mark, who quit his job in banking to take over the business. He also gave up his flat and moved into the flat above the bar."

"And now he drinks too much every night and then wanders up to bed after the bar closes," Charles said.

Andrew shook his head. "Actually, he told Nolan that he hasn't had a drink since the night of the murder. He said he can't shake the guilt that he feels that he didn't wake up and manage to stop Doug from getting killed."

"Interesting," Harry said.

"He took over the bar about ten years ago. Since then, he's had the entire building renovated. He's also purchased several other properties in the area. He now owns three bars, two restaurants, and a small hotel."

"My goodness," Bessie said. "He has been working hard."

Andrew nodded. "He's very successful, but Nolan said he's slightly less arrogant than he used to be, in spite of his success."

"We never asked about the order in which Nolan put the suspects," Harry said. "Was Mark at the top of his list? And if he was, is he still?"

"Mark was the top of his list. Then Rusty, then Tina, and finally Patti. That list hasn't changed over the years," Andrew replied.

"So Mark is nicer, but still his number-one suspect," Harry said.

"Does that mean that everyone is nicer now?" Doona asked.

"I very much doubt that," Harry said.

Everyone chuckled.

"Working down our list of suspects, then, does anyone want to speculate on where Rusty is now?"

"He's either still working as a waiter, or Doug's death

inspired him to go back to school and do something splendid with his life," Doona said.

"I think he's still a waiter," Hugh said. "He's probably still single. I doubt his life has changed much since the murder."

"Doona wins this time," Andrew said. "After Doug's death, Rusty decided to go back to school. He's now working as a science teacher for a high school in the suburbs of the city."

"Science is an interesting choice," Bessie said. When everyone looked at her, she shrugged. "I find it interesting, anyway."

Andrew grinned. "It is interesting. The first time he went to university, he studied business administration, but he told Nolan that he'd gone back because he wanted to make a difference in people's lives and that teaching was the most impactful way to do that."

"Good for him," Doona said.

"Is he married?" Hugh asked.

"He is married. His wife is also a high school teacher, but she teaches English."

"The American version," Charles said with a grin.

"Indeed," Andrew said. "They've been married for four years, and they have a two-year-old son. He's called Douglas."

"He named his son after his murdered friend," Hugh said. "I'm not certain if that's nice or if it's creepy."

Bessie shivered. "I find it creepy, but I suppose he might have thought of it as a way of keeping the memory of his friend alive."

"Or maybe he did it to try to assuage some of the guilt that he feels for having killed his friend," Hugh said.

"He's still second on Nolan's list," Harry said. "I'm looking forward to reading the statements and seeing how I feel about each of the suspects after I've done so."

"Any thoughts on Tina?" Andrew asked.

"She'll still be bitter and angry at the world," Charles said.

"She's probably still upset that she missed out on her chance to get closer to Mark, especially now that he's so successful."

Andrew nodded. "Right on all counts. She's been working as a waitress in a small café in a not-great part of the city for the past five years. When Nolan spoke to her last, about a year ago, he said that she seemed to blame everything that has gone wrong in her life on Doug, or rather on his murder."

"To be fair, her life wasn't that great before the murder," Doona said. "She complained about it constantly in her first interview."

"Yes, but, according to her, being involved in a murder investigation made it impossible for her to find work. The local papers covered the murder extensively, including publishing pictures of the four suspects. According to Tina, people avoided her on the street, and she got turned down for every job for which she applied for over a year."

"I find that difficult to believe," Harry said.

"Nolan pushed her a bit, getting her to admit that she'd only actually applied for a few jobs during that year and that some of those jobs were a considerable stretch, considering her lack of qualifications. She told Nolan that she'd given up applying after she'd realised that the murder investigation had made her unemployable, but it seems more likely that she didn't put much effort into the job hunt."

"How did she live if she wasn't working?" Doona asked.

"She was still staying with friends," Andrew replied. "They put up with her for an entire year before they finally kicked her out. She's bitter about that, too, of course."

"What did she do after they kicked her out?"

"She found a job tending bar. The bar wasn't in the best area, but it had a small flat above it that came with the job."

"But she isn't still there?"

"No, after a few years, the owners decided to sell the

place. The new owners closed the bar and turned the entire building into luxury flats. Tina moved around from job to job for a while, again staying with friends, but never anywhere for more than a few months. That goes for both her jobs and her living situation."

"I'm going to guess that she was drinking quite a lot in those days," Harry said.

Andrew nodded. "She admitted as much to Nolan in her most recent interview. Eventually, she decided that she needed to stop working in bars and found a job as a waitress in a coffee shop. She didn't stop drinking, but she slowed down a lot. After a few years there, she moved to the café where she's working now. She has her own flat now, too. It's what they call an efficiency apartment. Basically, it's one large room with an attached bathroom. According to Nolan, she complained a lot about having to live in one tiny room, especially when her former friends and fellow suspects are all living comfortably."

"How big is the flat over Mark's bar?" Harry asked.

"Remember that he had the building renovated," Andrew replied. "As part of the renovations, he had the flat extended over two floors. It's a five-storey building. The floors above the bar contained office space, aside from the one small flat. Now the flat takes up two entire floors. The rest is still office space."

"And Rusty's house must be larger than Tina's tiny flat," Doona said.

"Rusty and his wife live in a new subdivision full of large homes," Andrew said. "They are mortgaged to the hilt, but they have a lot of space."

"What did Tina have to say about Mark?" Bessie asked. "You said she was still upset that she'd never had a chance to get close to him on the camping trip."

Andrew nodded. "She told Nolan that she was certain he

was falling for her by the time they all went to bed on the night of the murder. She seems to think that she and Mark would be together now if the murder hadn't happened."

"He did have a girlfriend," Bessie said.

"And he didn't sound very keen on her in his interviews," Hugh added.

"She told Nolan that, after the murder, Mark told her that she was a reminder of the most awful thing that had ever happened to him," Andrew said.

Bessie winced. "That's harsh. Even if it's true, surely Mark could have found a nicer way to put it."

"For what it is worth, Mark denies ever saying any such thing to Tina. When Nolan asked him about the comment, he said he didn't remember saying much of anything to Tina after the murder. While Tina could list a half-dozen or so occasions when they'd seen one another after the murder, he said he didn't think he'd seen her more than once or twice in passing."

"Who is telling the truth?" John asked.

"In this instance, they both may be telling the truth," Andrew replied. "Many of the instances on Tina's list were nights in the bar when Mark was working. He may not have even noticed her, and it is possible that he went out of his way to avoid her."

"I'm sure that's what Tina thought was happening, anyway," Doona said.

"She did, indeed," Andrew replied.

"Were they ever asked who they thought killed Doug?" Bessie asked.

Andrew nodded. "Not in their initial interviews, but years later, yes. We can talk about their answers in a minute. I found them interesting."

"But first you want to talk about Patti," Doona said. "She was young and seemed very sweet. I hope she found a good job and a nice husband and is living happily somewhere with a handful of adorable children."

"Anyone else want to guess where Patti is now?" Andrew asked.

Bessie frowned. "While I thought she seemed sweet, I wouldn't be surprised if she'd done something shocking or unusual with her life. Maybe she joined the circus, or maybe she's been married a dozen times in the past twelve years."

"Bessie is closer to the truth," Andrew said.

Doona sighed. "I didn't get very much right, did I?"

"Patti has been married three times since the murder. Her first husband was the owner of the restaurant where she'd been working. They divorced only a year later, but Patti was given the restaurant in the divorce settlement. Two years later, she married one of the waiters she employed. They were only married for a few weeks before Patti filed for divorce. She then sold the restaurant and moved to Las Vegas."

"Las Vegas?" Doona echoed. "That's an interesting choice."

Andrew nodded. "She was there for a few years before she moved back to Pittsburgh. From what Nolan can determine, she was still living off the money she'd received when she'd sold the business. Last year, she got married again. Her third husband is wealthy, eighty-seven, and in poor health. He's also childless, which means Patti will probably inherit a great deal when he passes away."

"So she isn't as sweet as she seemed," Doona said.

"Maybe she genuinely loves the guy," Hugh said.

Doona looked at him. "Do you really think that's likely?"

Hugh laughed. "Not likely, but it may be possible."

"Nolan hasn't spoken to her for a year, but he did check that they are still together before he sent me the updates. When he interviewed her a year ago, they'd only been married for a few days. He said he's looking forward to finding out how married life is treating her."

"I'm sure it's hard work," Doona said. "I can't imagine having to pretend to care about someone for an entire year."

"Let's hope she really does care, then," Bessie said.

"Does any of that make her seem more likely to have been the killer?" Harry asked.

Bessie thought for a moment. "It suggests that she's not as innocent as she seemed. It also suggests that she's a talented actress, or at least willing to play a part."

Harry nodded. "She's still at the bottom of my list, but I'm going to read her updated statements very carefully. I'm more suspicious of her now than I was after I read the initial statements."

A few people nodded.

Andrew glanced at the clock. "I don't want to keep you all too much longer, but I do want to quickly go through what everyone said when they were asked who they thought killed Doug. Nolan asked the question when he spoke to each of them a year after the murder and then again when he spoke to them last year."

"It will be interesting to see who changed his or her answer," Harry said.

Andrew nodded. "We'll start with Mark again. The first time he was asked, he said it had to have been someone who'd hiked in from elsewhere. When Nolan told him that wasn't possible, he grudgingly said that it must have been Rusty, then. He told Nolan that Rusty and Doug had known each other for a really long time, so maybe Rusty had a reason to hate Doug."

"We haven't talked much about motive," Hugh said. "And I'm not sure I can come up with one for any of the suspects, really."

"It is difficult," Andrew agreed. "By all accounts, everyone in the group was friendly."

"We should talk about that," Bessie said. "What if Doug wasn't the intended victim?"

Andrew frowned. "Let's leave that conversation for later, after we've all had a chance to read the updates."

Bessie nodded and then made herself a note.

"Did Mark change his answer years later?" Harry asked.

Andrew shook his head. "If anything, he doubled down on his choice. He told Nolan that he tried not to think about the murder at all, but, when he did, he often wondered about the relationship between Rusty and Doug. He claimed, eleven years after the murder, that he could sense some tension between them before the murder."

"Interesting, and suspicious," Doona said. "If he'd said it the day after the murder, I might have believed him."

"No one else mentioned any tension between Rusty and Doug, at least not in their initial interviews," Hugh said.

Andrew nodded. "And, from what Nolan told me, no one else mentioned it later, either, aside from Mark. But let's move on to Rusty."

"Surely the others all just blamed Mark," Doona said.

Andrew chuckled. "You'd expect so, really, wouldn't you? And you'd be right – for Rusty, at least. A year after the murder, he told Nolan that Mark was the only suspect who made sense. Rusty couldn't suggest a motive, but he speculated that maybe Mark just wanted to see how it felt to kill someone."

"What a horrible thought," Bessie said with a shudder.

"I assume none of the suspects have ever been involved in any other murder investigations," Harry said.

"They have not. Nolan keeps a pretty close eye on all of them. Mark has had to ring the police once or twice at the bar, but he's the only one who has had any interaction with the police since the murder."

"And what did Rusty say a year ago?" Bessie asked after making a note.

"Much the same thing," Andrew told her. "Nolan said he seemed less certain, but he still said that Mark was the only answer that made sense."

"What about Tina?" Doona asked. "I can imagine her suggesting that Doug killed himself, just to ruin her life."

Andrew grinned. "She didn't say that, but she did insist that the killer had to have been someone from outside the campsite. She gave Nolan a long list of people who she claimed hated her and would have killed Doug just to upset her. That was at the interview a year after the murder. When Nolan asked her why she hadn't given him the list sooner, she said it had taken her a while to realise what must have happened."

"I hope Nolan didn't do anything with the list," Doona said.

"He did the right thing and checked for alibis for every name on it," Andrew told her. "All but one person had an alibi."

"That seems odd to me," Bessie said.

"It's less odd when you consider that all of the people on the list lived in Pittsburgh and the murder took place over three hours away," Andrew replied. "The killer would have had to drive all the way to the Forest and then hike to the camp, kill Doug, and then hike back out and drive home. If someone on the list could prove where he or she had been the night before the killing or early the next morning, that person was able to be eliminated."

"What about the one person who didn't have an alibi?" Doona asked.

"Nolan asked him a few questions but considered it highly unlikely that he had anything to do with the case. The man admitted that he knew that Tina was going camping that weekend but claimed that he had no idea where she was going. He told Nolan that he'd never been to the Allegheny National Forest, and he only had a vague idea of where it even was."

"I assume Nolan told Tina that he thought it was unlikely that someone from outside the campsite killed Doug," Harry said.

"He did. When pressed, Tina suggested that Rusty might have done it. She said she barely knew Rusty, which apparently made him the most likely suspect."

"And what did she say last year?" Doona asked.

"Last year she said she'd spent a lot of time thinking about it and she'd realised that Mark must have done it."

"A woman scorned," Doona murmured.

"Perhaps. She told Nolan that Mark was pretty much an outsider in their group and that he'd probably been jealous of Doug and how well liked he was."

"That seems a very weak motive for murder," Hugh said.

Andrew nodded. "Nolan said as much to Tina, but she just shrugged and said that she was entitled to her opinion."

"And that just leaves Patti," John said.

"In the first instance, Patti insisted that it had to have been a random stranger. She told Nolan that the people on the camping trip were her friends and that she wouldn't believe that any of them were capable of murder."

"And when he pressed her?" Hugh asked.

"She burst into tears and refused to answer."

"That's disappointing," Charles said.

"I hope she was more forthcoming last year," Harry said.

"She was. Last year, when Nolan asked again, she sighed

and said she'd been waiting for the question. Then she said that she'd thought about it a lot, but she hadn't been able to choose between Mark and Rusty. She said she assumed that Doug had had a disagreement with one of them after they'd all gone into their tents, but she wasn't certain which."

Bessie looked up from her notes. "Surely, if they were arguing in the tent, all three men were involved, at least to some extent."

Andrew shrugged. "Patti couldn't explain how two of the men could have argued without anyone else at the camp knowing, but at least she offered an opinion."

"And now to read everything else that everyone said," Harry said. He got to his feet and waited while Andrew found his envelope. "Thanks," he said as he took it. "I'll see you all in two days."

Charles left right behind him.

"Should we have dinner together tomorrow night?" Bessie asked the others as Andrew handed out their envelopes.

"Yes, please," Doona said. "I already want to talk about the case with all of you, and I haven't even read the updates yet."

"It's always nice to have an informal meeting in between the formal ones," John said.

"I'm not going to be able to be there," Andrew said. "I'm having dinner with the Chief Constable."

"I'll make notes if anything comes up that we want you to take back to Nolan," Bessie promised.

"I'll bring dinner and pudding," Hugh said. "The restaurant across from the station is still doing homestyle meals."

"Their food was very good," Bessie said. "I'll look forward to having it again."

With their plans made, John and Doona headed out. Hugh stopped to fill a takeaway box with biscuits while Bessie and Andrew packed up their things.

"See you tomorrow night," Bessie told Hugh as they parted company in the car park a few minutes later.

"See you tomorrow," Hugh replied.

CHAPTER 7

"Since I can't join you for dinner tomorrow night, maybe we can talk about the case later today," Andrew said as he drove them back towards Laxey.

Bessie looked at the thick envelope on her lap. "Later today?"

He grinned. "We can wait and talk tomorrow, if you prefer. I did think maybe we could spend some time tomorrow enjoying the island, though."

"Maybe we could go into Douglas," Bessie replied thoughtfully. "And maybe you could spend some time in the Manx Museum while I do a bit of research in the archives."

"What are you researching?"

"My cottage. I'm trying to find out when and why my cottage got its name."

"And you think the archives in the Museum might have that information?"

"I'm hoping they will. There are a number of different sources that I can search. I know the name of the couple from whom I purchased the cottage. I simply need to work backwards to try to find a widow who lived there."

"Could I be of any help to you?"

"Maybe, if you wanted to spend an hour poking around old documents and microfilm."

"It sounds as if it would be a fascinating way to spend an hour."

"I really should be spending all of my time on the case, though."

"You have the rest of this afternoon and all evening to work on the case. If we spend the morning in Douglas doing some research, I can bring you home right after lunch. That will give you all of tomorrow afternoon to do more work on the case before your dinner with Hugh, Doona, and John."

"And this time I don't have over a hundred witnesses to worry about," Bessie added, thinking about their last case.

"Nolan has interviewed the four witnesses multiple times over the past twelve years, but even so, it shouldn't take you a terribly long time to read all of the reports."

"If nothing else comes up, then, let's plan on that for tomorrow," Bessie said as Andrew parked the car next to her cottage.

"Would you like to take a stroll on the beach before you start working?" Andrew asked.

"I would, actually."

Andrew nodded. "It's a lovely afternoon. All I could think about during the meeting was getting back to Laxey and walking on the beach."

Bessie put her bag with the case file and the new envelope in her cottage and then changed into more comfortable shoes for walking. Then she went and sat on the rock behind her cottage. Andrew joined her a minute later.

"I need new shoes," he said as they began their stroll.

Bessie looked at his feet. "What's wrong with those shoes?"

"Nothing at all. I need new work shoes. The ones I wore to the meeting today seem to have given me a blister."

"Are they new?"

"Yes, and I probably should have tried them on before I bought them. They're the same shoes I always buy, and in the same size, too. I simply assumed that they would fit properly."

The pair chatted about shoes and sizes while they walked to Thie yn Traie and back.

"I needed that," Bessie said as they reached Andrew's cottage. "That's cleared my head. I'm ready to work now."

He nodded. "I'm looking forward to reading the updates. Will you be ready for dinner at six or would you prefer to go a bit later?"

Bessie looked at her watch. "Why don't we meet at your car at half six," she suggested. "That gives me a bit more time to read through the updated statements."

"Helen will undoubtedly be coming with us, so we won't be able to talk about the case over dinner."

"But we can talk after, at least until she comes to collect you."

Andrew laughed. "Maybe if I eat all of my vegetables at dinner, she'll let me stay up a bit later tonight."

Bessie gave him a hug and then watched as he let himself into his cottage. He appeared to be moving more easily today, but she still found herself worrying about him as she walked the short distance home. She made herself a cup of tea and then curled up with her case file.

By six-fifteen, she was ready for a break. She took the case file up to her office and locked it in a desk drawer. Then she changed into a nice dress for dinner. When she joined Andrew and Helen at his car, Andrew smiled.

"You've dressed up," he said. "We shall have to go somewhere nice."

"Not at all. I thought putting on a dress might improve my mood."

"Oh? Are you okay?" Andrew asked quickly.

She nodded. "I'm fine, really, just frustrated with the case. I've read all of the updated statements, and I don't think I'm any closer to working out what really happened at that campground that night than I was before I'd read them."

"We can talk later," Andrew said, glancing at Helen.

Helen sighed. "You can talk in front of me. You know I'd never repeat anything you said to anyone. Having said that, if you'd rather, I can stay here and make myself something for dinner, and you two can go and get dinner and talk about the case as much as you'd like."

"No," Bessie said firmly. "The last thing I want to do right now is talk about the case. Let's go and get dinner and talk about anything and everything else instead."

"Where do you want to go?" Andrew asked as they got into the car.

"A new pub opened recently just outside of Ramsey," Bessie said. "I've been told the food is excellent."

"Give me directions," Andrew said.

Ten minutes later, the trio was sitting at a corner table in the dining room of the small pub. A fire was burning in the fireplace, which made the room feel warm and cosy. The menus were on the table.

Bessie read down the list, her mouth watering. "I want about six things," she said after she'd read the menu twice.

"I was thinking the same thing, but I'm going to have the chicken in garlic sauce because I keep coming back to it," Helen said.

Andrew sighed. "I was looking at that, but then I read down the list of pies. I think I'm going to have steak and kidney pie."

"I'll have the roast chicken dinner," Bessie decided. "It's

been ages since I roasted a chicken and I rarely fuss with all of the extras these days."

"And now that sounds good," Andrew said with a chuckle.

"It really does, but I do roast chickens pretty regularly at home," Helen said. "I'm going to stick to my first choice."

Andrew went to the bar to place their order. He brought them all fizzy drinks when he returned.

"I ordered the roast chicken," he said as he sat down. "I decided that I couldn't sit across from Bessie and watch her eat so many wonderful things and not have them myself."

They were discussing cooking techniques when their food arrived. Bessie's meal was everything she'd hoped it would be.

"Everything was wonderful," she told the waiter as he cleared their empty plates a short while later. "If I still cooked regularly, I'd be begging you for the recipe for those stuffing balls."

He grinned. "We get asked for it all the time. The chef always says no."

After some deliberation, Bessie decided on the sticky toffee pudding for pudding. Andrew got jam roly-poly, and Helen opted for a crème caramel.

"Delicious," Bessie said after her first bite.

"So is mine," Helen told her.

"Mine is terrible," Andrew said with a huge grin. "So don't even think about asking for a bite."

They all laughed and then finished their puddings happily before Andrew drove them back to Laxey Beach.

"And now you two want to talk about the case, and I want to curl up with a good book," Helen said as they got out of the car. "Dad, not too late."

Andrew made a face. "I won't be too late, but you've no need to wait up for me."

She grinned at him. "You know I won't go to bed until the

killer is caught. That's the joy of fictional murders. The killer gets caught in a set number of pages."

"Unlike our case, which took place twelve years ago," Andrew said.

Helen frowned. "That's a very long time for someone to get away with murder."

Andrew and Bessie walked to her cottage, and she unlocked the door. Inside, Andrew quickly checked things over while Bessie put the kettle on. Then they sat together at the kitchen table with their tea.

"Where should we start?" Andrew asked.

Bessie sighed. "I wish I knew. I'm struggling with motive, and all four of the suspects had the means and the opportunity. They all talk about how Doug kept his knife in a sheath on his belt for most of the day before taking it off and sticking it in a tree just outside of his tent before they went to bed that night. He told them that he was leaving it there in case anyone needed it for protection."

"Which seems like a strange thing to do," Andrew said.

"I thought so, but I know nothing about camping."

"Whether it was strange or not, all of the suspects agreed that he did it, and Rusty said that Doug always left his knife nearby when they went to bed."

"Nearby, right where a killer could grab it," Bessie said.

"You said something in the meeting today about wondering if Doug was the intended victim."

Bessie shrugged. "I probably only wondered because of our last case. We had three bodies and only one of them was the killer's actual target. It doesn't seem as if anyone had any reason to want to kill Doug, so I started to wonder if anyone had any reason to kill any of the others."

Andrew thought for a minute. "I would suggest that Mark was the least-liked member of the group."

"But not liking someone is a long way away from killing

him. Even if they found him annoying or horrible, they were all going home the next day. Once they got back to the city, they could have all avoided one another, surely?"

"Doug had to put up with Mark if he was going to keep his job," Andrew said. "And Tina worked at the bar occasionally."

"But she didn't have to work there. She gave Nolan a list of three or four other places where she also sometimes worked behind the bar."

"Let's take things in some sort of order. Doug presumably didn't want to kill anyone."

"I suppose we could argue that he tried to kill someone, and that person turned the knife on him in self-defense."

"Except there was no sign of any disturbance. The evidence suggests that Doug was asleep or at least resting in his sleeping bag when he was stabbed."

"Should we talk about suspects or potential victims, then?"

"Let's talk about potential victims. What if the killer thought he or she was killing Mark?"

"Then I suspect Tina," Bessie said quickly. "Maybe she told him how she felt and he rejected her without her ever realising that she was talking to the wrong man."

"That's certainly one possibility. Can you think of a motive for anyone else?"

"I can think of motives for all of them, but they get increasingly unlikely. Maybe Rusty thought Mark was interfering with his friendship with Doug. Maybe Mark behaved inappropriately with Patti. There are any number of possibilities."

"But they all seemed to be getting along the next day when the police arrived," Andrew said.

"I think if I'd accidentally killed the wrong man that I'd

do everything in my power to be nice and kind to everyone else in the group the next day."

"Which rules out Tina, then," Andrew suggested.

Bessie shook her head. "Just because that is what I would do doesn't mean anything."

"So what if Rusty was the intended victim?" Andrew asked.

Bessie frowned. "I suppose Mark might have had some reason for wanting him dead, but I'm not sure what it could be. Both of the women seemed to get along with Rusty quite well."

Andrew nodded. "They both said he was a nice guy and a good friend."

"So if Rusty was the intended victim, Mark must have killed him."

"Unless the killer just wanted to kill someone."

"Which is a horrible thing to consider."

"Maybe the killer woke up and saw Doug in the third tent and panicked, thinking it was an intruder."

"That's a better idea," Bessie said. "But if that was what happened, why not say so the next morning? Or, better yet, why not start screaming and wake up the entire campsite rather than stabbing a stranger to death?"

Andrew nodded. "Did anyone have a motive for killing Tina?"

"She seemed annoying, but lots of people are annoying."

"She'd turned up late that morning, but they hadn't actually waited for her. I can't see any of them being angry enough to kill her over that."

"Maybe one of the men wanted to, um, get friendly with her, and she turned him down."

"I would imagine she wouldn't have turned down Mark. I'm not certain I can see Rusty wanting to kill someone for turning him down."

Bessie sighed. "Maybe she and Patti had a fight. Maybe one of them got angry enough to decide to go and sleep in the other tent. Maybe, after that woman stormed off, the other woman went after her to kill her."

"That almost makes sense, but where did the first woman go? When she got to the third tent, she'd have found Doug inside. What then?"

Bessie thought for a moment. "Then she decided to take a short walk to clear her head. While she was off walking, the second woman sneaked into the third tent and stabbed Doug to death, thinking she was killing the first woman. Then she went back to their tent and went back to sleep."

"And the first woman, having walked off her anger, went back to the women's tent, too, eventually."

"Yes, which probably shocked the killer, but she couldn't very well say anything."

Andrew took a sip of tea. "It's possible," he said as he put his cup down. "We'd just have to work out which woman was the first woman and which was the second."

"I suppose it could have happened either way, but if it did happen, why didn't either woman mention the disagreement the next day? I mean, it's obvious why the killer didn't mention it, but why didn't the other woman?"

"That's what makes the story seem unlikely. All of the stories we've discussed seem unlikely, really, but we still don't know why anyone wanted Doug dead."

Bessie sighed. "I read the autopsy and the police report several times, but I'm not sure I understood it all. Doug was stabbed through his sleeping bag. The report seemed to say that they thought it was unlikely that any of his blood got on the killer."

Andrew nodded. "Doug was inside a waterproof sleeping bag when he was stabbed. The knife cut through the bag, but the bag held most if not all of the blood, at least initially. The police believe that the killer had time to get away before blood started seeping through the holes that the knife had left in the bag."

"How dreadful," Bessie said.

Andrew opened his mouth to reply, but he was interrupted by his mobile.

"Hello?" After a short pause, he sighed and then spoke again. "I'll be there in five minutes," he said.

"Is something wrong?" Bessie asked as Andrew quickly drank the last of his tea.

"That was Helen. There's a small family matter that needs some attention. I suspect it's much ado about nothing, but Helen has happily seized on it as a means to getting me back to the cottage nice and early."

"I don't know that we were getting anywhere anyway," Bessie said.

"But I was enjoying the conversation."

"Do you still want to go into Douglas tomorrow morning?"

"Yes, of course. We can talk about the case again after lunch. Let's have an enjoyable morning."

"Helen has to work, I assume."

"Yes, she does, but I'm not sure she'd be excited about a morning in the archives anyway."

"I'm surprised you are."

Andrew chuckled. "I'm retired, or mostly retired. An afternoon of poking at old documents is just about the right level of excitement for me."

Bessie walked him to the door and then gave him a hug.

"The Museum and the archives open at ten," she told him.

"I'll be ready to leave at half nine."

"Perfect."

She watched him walk back to his cottage and then shut and locked the door. It was too early for her to head to bed, so she washed the teacups and then stood in the centre of her sitting room and tried to decide what to do next.

"I should look at the case file," she said softly. "Or I could read a book."

Grabbing the book from the table next to her favourite chair, Bessie headed up the stairs. Once she was comfortable under the duvet, she opened the book and started to read. Half an hour later, she slammed the book shut and only just resisted the urge to throw it across the room.

"It simply doesn't make sense," she complained loudly. "I could drive a bus though some of the plot holes, and I don't even know how to drive. The main character is one of the most annoying people I've ever read about. The other characters are boring and predictable. Every character in the story had a motive for wanting the victim dead, but he was killed by a knife that was supposed to have been locked in a safe and was completely inaccessible. Obviously, the author is going to have to pull a rabbit out of her hat to fix that, but even if the knife suddenly fell from the sky, the victim was allegedly alone in the house on the night of the murder. A security team was patrolling the property. There were cameras everywhere. Maybe that's it. Maybe the knife truly did just fall from the sky, right into the victim's chest, where it then jumped up and down several times before settling."

Rant over, Bessie went to the loo and got herself a glass of water. After a few sips, she started to feel a bit better. As she climbed back into bed, she glanced over at the book. "Tomorrow, I'm just going to read the ending," she whispered. "I've never, ever just read the beginning and the ending of a story, but I'm going to make an exception just this once."

The idea made her feel much better. She switched off the light and then rolled over and went to sleep.

CHAPTER 8

Bessie wasn't any less grumpy when she woke up the next morning. She muttered to herself as she got ready for the day, casting angry glances at the book on her bedside table as she did so. After carrying the book downstairs, she put it on the table in the kitchen.

"When I get back from my walk, I'm going to read the last chapter," she told the book. "And I expect to be disappointed, even with my low expectations."

A brisk walk on the beach worked its usual magic. When Bessie got back to her cottage, she was feeling far less cross with the world. She made herself some toast with honey and strawberry jam and then cut an apple into bite-sized pieces. After making tea, she sat down with her breakfast and the book.

"Good morning," Andrew said when she met him at his car at half nine.

"Good morning," she replied.

He raised an eyebrow. "You don't sound happy."

Bessie chuckled. "Is it that obvious?"

"Is everything okay?"

"Oh, yes, everything is fine, really. I read the most dreadful book, although I didn't read all of it."

"Oh? Did you stop halfway through?"

"Yes, and then I read the last chapter."

Andrew grinned. "I take it the last chapter wasn't any better than the rest." He unlocked the car and opened Bessie's door for her. Once she was safely inside, he shut her door and then walked around and got in behind the steering wheel. As he started the engine, Bessie replied.

"No, the last chapter was not any better than the rest. A man was stabbed to death in his bed while he was alone inside a house that was supposedly well guarded. The knife used for the murder was supposed to have been locked in a safe that no one was able to access. There were over a dozen suspects to try to keep track of, all of whom had strong motives but none of whom had the means or the opportunity."

"Surely the killer was found in the end?"

"Yes, because in the very last chapter it was revealed that there was a secret entrance to the house that only one person knew about. That person also knew the combination to the safe, which had been lost thirty years earlier, even though that person was only twenty-three at the time of the murder." Bessie blew out a sigh. "And that person, who'd only been in the village for three weeks and wasn't really even considered a suspect, turned out to be the victim's long-lost son, even though the victim had been told as a child that he'd never be able to father children."

Andrew frowned. "How did the long-lost son know about the secret entrance?"

"I can give you the author's name. You can write to her and ask her. She certainly didn't bother to explain that in the book."

"I am sorry. Badly written books annoy me no end, too."

"I'm just glad that I didn't buy the second book in the series. I'm rather torn, though, as to what to do with the book now. I usually donate books that I don't want to keep to one of the charity shops, but I really don't want anyone to read this one."

"I can take it back to London, and donate it to a charity shop there," Andrew offered. "At least then no one you know will buy it."

"That isn't a bad idea. I hate the thought of throwing away a book, even one as badly written as this one. I'll have to think about it, though. I'm not sure the good people of London should have to suffer."

While they'd been talking, Andrew had been driving. As they reached the outskirts of Douglas, Bessie shook her head.

"I hope Helen has a good day at work today," she said, determined to change the subject and put the book out of her head.

Andrew nodded. "She may only work for half the day. She was talking about driving her hire car into Ramsey and doing some shopping later."

They chatted about the shops in Ramsey as Andrew found a parking space in the small multi-storey car park near the Manx Museum. It was one minute to ten when they reached the back door to the museum. A young historian that Bessie knew was pacing just outside the door.

"Good morning," Bessie said.

"Ah, good morning," the young man replied.

"Eager to get to work?" she asked.

He grinned. "I found the most fascinating document in a random box yesterday. Sadly, it was two minutes before the Museum closed for the day, so I only got a very quick look at it. It isn't at all what I was looking for, but now I can't wait to read it properly and then see what else is in the box."

Behind them, the large wooden door slowly swung open. Bessie smiled as the young man ran up the steps and disappeared into the building. She and Andrew followed more slowly. Marjorie waved as Bessie walked into the library.

"I wasn't expecting you here this week," she said as Bessie and Andrew approached the counter.

Bessie quickly introduced the pair. "We had a free morning, so I thought I'd come and see if I could find anything interesting," she explained.

"I couldn't resist doing a bit of poking around," Marjorie said. "Your sellers, Ewan and Margaret Christian, bought the cottage from a Joney Carlson about ten years before you bought the cottage."

"Just Joney? She wasn't married?" Bessie asked.

"The listing only gave her name, nothing more, but the property was identified as Treoghe Bwaane at that time."

"Interesting. Do you have the date of the sale?"

Marjorie pulled a small notebook out of her pocket and flipped through the pages. Then she read out a date to Bessie.

Bessie made a note in her own notebook. "I wonder if we could find more in the local paper," she said. "Sometimes, on slow news days, they used to give additional information about property sales."

Marjorie nodded. "That was going to be my suggestion. You have the date, so you know exactly where to look."

"And the papers are all on microfilm," Bessie sighed. "Are the machines all booked for today?"

Marjorie checked the schedule on the desk behind her and then smiled at Bessie. "We had a cancellation, actually. It's only for an hour, but you can use a machine from now until eleven. I'll get you the film for that date."

"We shouldn't need an hour, should we?" Andrew asked.

Bessie shrugged. "Usually, the papers go nicely in order

by date, but some of the films were done a bit more haphazardly, which makes it more difficult to find things. Even if we can find the right date easily, though, we may struggle to find the article on property sales. It usually gets tucked in wherever they have the right-size space."

"I'm surprised there's that much demand for microfilm machines," Andrew said as they watched multiple people going into the small room that held the machines.

"There are a limited number of machines, and a great deal of the island's records are held on film. Anyone doing family history research needs a machine to go through the parish registers, for example. And the island has quite a few researchers who do family histories for people elsewhere in the world."

"Really?"

Bessie nodded. "The requests mostly come from America. A great many Manx men and women emigrated there, including my own family, of course. Apparently, a lot of younger men and women are now taking a keen interest in their heritage."

Marjorie was back a moment later with the roll of microfilm. "According to the notes in the back, this film is a bit mixed up. The dates go in order for a while and then get a bit scrambled. I hope you can find what you want without too much trouble."

"We'll find it," Bessie said. "We may not find it in this hour, though."

"You go and get started. I'll see if we can move a few people around to give you some extra time."

"I don't want to be a bother," Bessie said.

Marjorie nodded. "I won't promise anything. You go and get to work."

Andrew followed Bessie into the room that held a row of

microfilm machines. Bessie took the only empty seat and then waved at the chairs against the opposite wall.

"You can pull up a chair," she told Andrew in a low voice.

He nodded, and carefully and quietly carried one of the chairs over and put it next to Bessie's. She was slowly inserting the film into the machine. Then she began to scroll through the film, checking every so often for the date.

"Ah," she said excitedly a few minutes later. "We're getting close."

She scrolled a bit farther and then sighed. "And now we aren't."

"What's happened?" Andrew asked.

"The papers jumped a month, and now they seem to be all over the place. I'll have to scroll more slowly and check every page, I suppose."

Twenty minutes later, Bessie's head was starting to hurt. She sat back and shut her eyes.

"It's hard work, isn't it?" the woman next to her said.

Bessie nodded. "I'm out of practise. And the newspapers are worse than the parish registers. At least the parish registers are in the correct order."

"Shall I have a go?" Andrew asked.

Bessie looked at the film on the machine. "I'm only about halfway through the film, so we've a long way to go. If you want to have a turn, please do."

She slid her chair sideways a bit to let Andrew move forwards. Then she sat back and closed her eyes again. Two minutes later, Andrew spoke again.

"I think I've found it."

Bessie frowned and sat up. "Already? That hardly seems fair." While she was eager to find the correct newspaper, she was almost hoping that Andrew was mistaken. He was not, though. He'd found the paper from the right date.

Now Bessie took back over, slowly reading through each

section of each page of the paper, trying to find the article she wanted. She found more than she'd been expecting on the second page.

"'Island Widow Sells Cottage,'" Bessie read the headline.

"Is it your cottage?" Andrew asked.

Bessie quickly skimmed the article, which included listings for multiple sales across the island.

"Here it is. 'Joney Carlson has sold her cottage to her sister and brother-in-law,'" she read. "Ewan and Margaret Christian purchased the cottage on Laxey Beach, now called Treoghe Bwaane, almost exactly ten years after Joney's husband, Joseph, passed away unexpectedly. Joney refused to comment when asked about the sale.'"

"Well, there you are, then," Andrew said.

"What happened to her husband?" Bessie asked. "Why doesn't the article give any additional information?"

"Maybe we need to look at newspapers from ten years earlier."

"Yes, I expect we do."

Bessie inserted coins to get a copy of the page she was viewing, then rewound the film and put it back in its box.

"I'm going to ask for the films for three months on either side of the date," Bessie said, reaching for a request slip. "We'll start with a week on either side and keep working backwards. I just hope the papers are in the correct order in these films."

Andrew took the film they'd used and the request slips to the desk. He was back a few minutes later with three boxes of film.

"Marjorie asked me to tell you that we have twenty minutes left," he said as he handed her the films.

Bessie glanced at the clock. "So she got us a few extra minutes, at least," she said. "I wish I knew where to start."

"Start with the first of the month ten years before the sale," Andrew suggested.

"I wish I knew what I was looking for," Bessie said a few minutes later. "The man's death might not have been considered newsworthy at the time."

She scrolled carefully through the papers, reading every headline, searching for anything relevant.

"We only have one more minute," Andrew said eventually. "And I think the person waiting for our machine is here."

Bessie glanced back and smiled at the young woman who was standing behind them. She glanced at the clock and then looked back at Bessie.

Sighing, Bessie scrolled forward. "Just one more page," she told Andrew. "Then I'll make a note of where we stopped so we know where to start next time."

She finished reading the page and then made a note. "That was the last page of that paper. Next time we come, we'll start with the headlines from the next day."

As she spoke, she scrolled forwards again, stopping as the next day's front page filled the screen.

"Man Found Dead on Laxey Beach," the headline screamed at her.

Bessie gasped. "Or maybe we've found it," she exclaimed.

The woman behind her coughed loudly.

Andrew dug a few coins out of his pocket and dropped them into the machine. It whirred quietly as it made a copy of the page on the screen. When it was finished, Bessie checked quickly to be certain that the article wasn't continued elsewhere in the paper. There was nothing at the end of the piece to suggest that it had been, anyway. Sighing, Bessie quickly rewound the film and then removed it from the machine. As she and Andrew gathered their things, the woman behind them moved forwards. She was in Bessie's seat, loading her microfilm, before Andrew and Bessie made it to the door.

"Did you find anything interesting?" Marjorie asked as Bessie handed back the films.

"I think so," Bessie said. "But at the very end of our time, so we just made a copy. I haven't read it yet."

"I wish I could hear more, but I'm already late for a meeting," Marjorie said. She rushed out of the room before Bessie could reply.

"We need more time with a microfilm machine," Bessie said.

She was talking to Andrew, but the young woman behind the counter frowned and picked up the schedule on the desk.

"We don't have any times available today. The next available spot is at three tomorrow afternoon," she told Bessie.

"Which is when we have our meeting," Bessie said.

"What about the next day?" Andrew asked.

"I have an hour at ten or an hour at four," the woman replied.

"Can we have them both?" was Andrew's next question.

"I'm sorry, but researchers are limited to a single hour each day, unless they're working on certain projects. We do our best to make certain that everyone has a chance to use the archives."

Bessie nodded. "We'll take the ten o'clock hour. Thank you."

The woman wrote her name neatly on the schedule. "Do you want the same films back again?" she asked.

Bessie nodded. "I think we only need one of them." She pointed to the film she'd just removed from the machine.

"We'll have the film out when you arrive," the woman told her. "It will be in the tray by the door as you come in. You can just take it and get started on machine four."

"Thank you," Bessie said.

She walked out of the library and then out of the building. Andrew followed. It wasn't until she was halfway to the car that she realised that he wasn't right behind her.

"Sorry," he said when he caught up. "You were walking rather quickly."

Bessie frowned. "I'm just very eager to read the page we copied. I didn't want to do it in the library, because I know we're going to want to talk about the story."

"I'm as excited as you are, just not as fast."

"Let's sit here and take a look," Bessie suggested, gesturing towards a nearby bench.

They sat together and Bessie pulled the sheet out of her bag.

"'Police were called to Laxey Beach this morning when a man walking his dog found a man lying dead on the sand in front of the row of cottages there,'" Bessie read aloud.

"It doesn't have to have been Joseph Carlson's body," Andrew said.

"I know it doesn't. I'm not sure I'd be that disappointed if it wasn't, at this point. I can't quite believe that I never knew that a body had been found on the beach all those years ago, though."

"Presumably, if it was murder, the police found the killer," Andrew said.

Bessie didn't answer. She'd gone back to reading the article. After a minute, she sighed and looked up at Andrew.

"This is just a very preliminary report," she said. "All they really know is that a body was found. They interviewed the man who found the body, but he just talks about how much his dog barked and what a surprise it was. If he knew the identity of the man, he didn't reveal it."

"Did he live on Laxey Beach?"

"No, he'd walked down from central Laxey so that his dog could walk on the beach. Apparently, his dog loved water, so, on weekends, when he had more time, he used to take him to the beach for his morning walk."

"What day of the week was the body found?" Andrew asked.

"It was a Saturday morning. The man said he arrived at the beach around six o'clock. The sun was just starting to rise. He said that as soon as they reached the beach, the dog started barking and pulling on his lead."

"So the dog led the man to the body?"

"According to the man, anyway."

"But he didn't say anything about what might have happened to the man?"

"Oh, he said plenty about that," Bessie said with a small laugh. "He offered all sorts of speculation, suggesting everything from a drunken accident to aliens."

"Aliens?"

Bessie held the sheet of paper out to Andrew, pointing to the section where the man had offered his thoughts on what might have happened.

"I hope the man wrote books in his spare time," Andrew said after he'd read the paragraph. "He had quite an imagination."

Bessie read through the article a second time. "I'm not certain how I can wait two more days to find out more. The man in question almost has to have been Joseph Carlson. If it is, though, did Joney become a widow because her husband was murdered on the beach outside of their home?"

"Maybe you should ring John and see if he can let us take a look at the police report on the incident," Andrew suggested.

"I doubt he'd let us do that."

"We could suggest that the cold case unit might consider the case."

Bessie chuckled. "The case must have been solved years ago. Otherwise, I'm certain I would have heard about it."

Andrew shrugged. "I can request the file directly from the Chief Constable tonight. I can't imagine he'd say no."

"I hate to say yes, but I'm too curious to refuse. Just don't do anything that might annoy the Chief Constable."

"I'm not the least bit worried about that," Andrew assured her.

CHAPTER 9

The pair had lunch at one of Bessie's favourite restaurants. While they chatted about several different subjects, Bessie was clearly distracted.

"You can't stop thinking about the body on the beach, can you?" Andrew asked while they were waiting for their pudding.

Bessie sighed. "Is it that obvious? I've been sitting here trying to think of anyone I know who might know more. It was too long ago, though."

"I was wondering if Joney and Joseph had any children."

"That's a good question," Bessie said. "Of course, that information will be in the parish registers, which are also on microfilm."

Andrew sighed. "I think our best option is to ask the Chief Constable for access to the police file."

"I just feel weird about asking him for favours. I wouldn't even have a chance to do so if it weren't for you."

"You aren't asking him for a favour. I am. I don't have any qualms about asking."

"I wonder if the *Isle of Man Times* keeps copies of all of its papers."

"You could ring Dan Ross and ask him."

Bessie made a face. "Or maybe I'll just wait until we can get back into the archives at the Museum."

After lunch, they spent an hour walking up and down the shopping street, looking in windows and visiting a few shops. They left the bookshop for last.

"I very nearly told the woman behind the counter to take the book I read last night off the shelf," Bessie said to Andrew as they made their way back to his car, each carrying a bag of books.

"I doubt she would have done it."

"She wouldn't have. I mentioned the book to her. Apparently, she loved it."

"She did?"

Bessie shook her head. "I was standing there, going through the mystery section, looking for something good, when she walked over and asked if she could help. I pointed to the book and said I'd just finished reading it. Before I could say anything more, she started to go on and on about how wonderful it was and how much she'd enjoyed it."

"Are you sure it was the same book?"

"Sadly, yes. She said she'd loved how the case seemed impossible but the detective managed to solve it anyway. She talked about the amazing twist that was the true identity of the killer. When I asked her how she thought he knew about the secret door, she just shrugged and said she didn't see why it mattered."

Andrew grinned. "Maybe it doesn't matter."

Bessie inhaled sharply. "The story needs to make sense."

"And it did, to your young friend."

"On the contrary, she realised that it didn't make sense. She simply didn't care."

They'd reached Andrew's hire car. He put all of the bags in his boot and then smiled at Bessie.

"I think you need a treat," he said.

"I had pudding with lunch."

"Does that mean you don't want ice cream?"

Bessie thought for a minute and then frowned. "I didn't want ice cream, right up until you mentioned it. Now I'd rather like some ice cream."

It didn't take them long to walk to the small ice cream shop nearby. Bessie got two scoops of vanilla. Andrew had one of chocolate and one of strawberry.

"And now the world feels much brighter," Bessie said as they walked back to the car again.

"I knew ice cream would cheer you up."

Andrew drove them back to Laxey. When he parked outside of Bessie's cottage, he frowned.

"Helen is out somewhere," he said.

Bessie looked around the otherwise empty parking area. "You did say that she was thinking of going to the shops this afternoon."

"Yes, I know, but I thought she'd be back by now."

The words were barely out of his mouth when another car suddenly appeared on the road next to the cottages. When it turned into the parking area for Bessie's cottage, she recognized Helen behind the wheel.

"And there she is," she said to Andrew.

He grinned. "Perfect timing. I'd almost suspect that she was watching for us so that I would have to help her unload the shopping."

Andrew opened his boot and Bessie quickly pulled out her shopping bags. After grabbing his and then shutting the boot, he walked over to Helen's car.

"I didn't buy much," Helen said as she emerged from the vehicle. "Just enough for a few days."

As she opened the boot, Bessie hid a smile. The boot was full of shopping bags, and Bessie suspected that she could live for a fortnight or longer on the supplies that Helen had purchased.

"Enjoy your dinner tonight," Bessie told Andrew. "I'll see you tomorrow."

"If my dinner ends early enough, I may come and see you later," Andrew replied. "I'm certain you and the others are going to come up with quite a few questions for Nolan."

"I wish I had your confidence, but if you see lights on in the cottage, you're more than welcome to come over."

As Helen and Andrew headed into their cottage, both carrying multiple shopping bags, Bessie made her way back to Treoghe Bwaane. As she opened her door, she stopped to run her fingers across the sign that had been there for many years.

"It isn't the original," she reminded herself as she pushed the door shut. After putting away the box of chocolate truffles she'd bought for an especially indulgent day in the future, Bessie sat down with her new books and selected one almost at random. She was still reading when someone knocked on her door just before six.

"John, Doona, hello," she said after she'd opened the door.

"Hello," Doona replied, giving Bessie a hug.

Bessie gave John a hug, too, and then closed the door behind them.

"Hugh might be a few minutes late," Doona said as she took a seat at the table. "The restaurant across from the station was shut when he went to get dinner."

"Shut? For good or just for tonight?"

Doona shrugged. "The sign just said 'closed,' with no explanation."

Bessie frowned. "I suppose we should have been

expecting it, really. They were there for at least a month, weren't they? That's a long time for that location."

"It is, but Hugh wasn't expecting it. He texted me and said he'd get food from somewhere and be here as soon as he could," Doona told her.

"If he can't get pudding, I have several boxes of biscuits," Bessie said. "And I think there is still some ice cream in my freezer from a few months ago when it sounded good."

She checked the freezer and found two tubs of ice cream. Feeling as if she had pudding well in hand, she sat at the table with Doona and John, chatting about Thomas and Amy, until Hugh finally arrived almost half an hour late.

"I'm sorry," were the first words out of his mouth when Bessie opened the door to his knock.

"It isn't your fault," Bessie said quickly.

"I still feel terrible. I left the station thinking I had plenty of time. I walked over to the restaurant, ready to collect my order, and it was shut."

"When did you order?" Bessie asked.

"Yesterday. I rang them and ordered everything I thought we could possibly want, plus a few extra things. I thought I could take the leftovers home to Grace. She's often too tired to cook these days."

"The poor girl," Bessie murmured.

"I'm just glad I didn't pay yesterday," Hugh said. "They offered to take my credit card details over the phone, but I said I'd pay when I collected the order."

"That was smart," Doona said.

Hugh flushed. "It wasn't, though. I just didn't have my wallet to hand. Otherwise, I would have given them my credit card information without a single thought."

"So where did you end up getting dinner from?" Bessie asked as Hugh began to unpack the box he'd carried into the cottage.

"I thought I'd go to the little Italian place, but they had a queue out the door waiting for tables, so I worried that takeaway would take ages. Then I thought I'd just get fish and chips at the chippy, but they were closed. The sign said they'd had a family emergency."

Bessie nodded. "I'm not certain I'd call a new baby an emergency – especially since, as far as I know, both mother and baby are doing well – but I can understand why the proud new father wanted a day or two off work."

"I understand, too, but I do wish she would have waited a few extra days to have that baby," Hugh said.

"So where did the food come from?" Doona asked as Bessie got down plates.

"Ah, right, so I was driving around, trying to work out where to go. I decided I might as well get something from the pub, so I headed there, but then I spotted a sign by the side of the road. You know the tiny little café near the Laxey Wheel?"

Bessie nodded. "I know the woman who used to run that café. She took over Dan's old building in Lonan."

"Yes, well, now someone has taken over her old building by the Wheel," Hugh said.

"That tiny building?" Doona asked. "There is only room for four tables, and I'm sure when I was there last that the cooker wasn't working."

Hugh shrugged. "There were six tables in the dining room, but none of them were occupied when I was there. The new owner said he's having trouble letting customers know that he's open for business."

"Did you get his name?" Bessie asked.

"Malcolm Smythe. He's only been on the island for a few weeks. Apparently he saw the sales listing for the café online and bought it without even coming over to see it."

"And then, when he did come over, he was hugely disappointed," Bessie guessed.

Hugh chuckled. "Yeah, he didn't come right out and say that, but it was obvious that the building wasn't what he'd been expecting. He's making the best of it, though. He had the old tables for four taken out and replaced them with tables for two. He also said he had the kitchen updated, but, from where I was standing, it didn't look very updated."

"How much of the kitchen could you see?" Doona asked.

"Quite a bit, actually. Malcolm had the wall between the kitchen and the dining room taken out, and then he replaced it with a series of screens. It makes the space feel bigger, but it also means that people in the café can see everything that happens in the kitchen."

"What is it?" Doona asked. She'd opened the first container and was frowning at its contents.

"That one is beef stew," Hugh told her. "Then there is grilled chicken with rice. The last one is bangers and mash in gravy."

Doona opened all three of the trays and then shrugged. "If you say so," she said. "Everything is rather grey."

Bessie took a small helping of all three dishes. None of it looked appealing, but it didn't smell unpleasant. Once everyone had taken what they wanted, Doona got them all drinks, and then they sat down at the table together.

"Did Malcolm have a restaurant wherever he was before he came here?" Bessie asked as she picked up her fork.

"He told me that he's worked in the restaurant business for over forty years, but he didn't specify what he'd done exactly," Hugh said, frowning over his plate. "Maybe he did the washing-up for forty years."

Bessie poked at a piece of what she thought was chicken and then decided to try the rice first. Everyone stared at her expectantly as she chewed and then swallowed.

"How was it?" Doona asked as Bessie reached for her drink.

"Not terrible," Bessie said. "It's plain white rice that could have been cooked for a bit longer, but it isn't awful."

Ten minutes later, everyone pushed their plates away.

"The stew wasn't dreadful," Hugh said.

"And the mashed potatoes were okay, as long as you don't mind powdered potatoes," John said.

"We ate them a lot when I was a kid," Doona said. "I actually like them. Well, I usually like them. These weren't great."

"They were quite lumpy," Bessie said, looking at her plate. "But they were still better than the sausages."

"I don't know where he got them from, but I hope he won't buy them again," Hugh said. "Not that I'm planning on getting food from there again, but no one should have to eat sausages like those."

"I hope you didn't get pudding from him," Doona said.

Hugh flushed. "I got a Victoria sponge. Because I'd purchased so much food, he gave me a good deal on an entire cake."

"Oh, good," Doona said faintly.

John and Hugh cleared the table.

"What do we do with the leftovers?" Hugh asked as he stared at the containers on the counter.

"Just throw them away," Bessie said. "I hate to waste food, but most of that wasn't edible anyway."

Once the counter was clear, Hugh opened the cake box. Everyone looked at the Victoria sponge.

"It looks good," Doona said after a moment.

"It really does," Bessie agreed. "In fact, it looks as if the bakery in Ramsey made it."

Hugh took it out of the box and put it on a plate. "It looks exactly the same as their cakes," he said. "Right down to the pattern in the icing sugar on top."

Doona cut everyone generous slices of cake. Bessie took one bite and grinned.

"Malcolm is buying his cakes from the bakery in Ramsey," she said. "And I'm exceedingly grateful for that."

Everyone enjoyed the cake a great deal more than they had the food. Once the cake plates had been cleared and Bessie had made tea, John cleared his throat.

"We're supposed to be talking about the case," he said.

"We'd usually have started by now, but the food distracted us," Doona said with a laugh.

"So where do we start?" Hugh asked.

"Motives?" Doona suggested. "We haven't really talked about motives yet."

"Probably because no one seemed to have an obvious one," Bessie said.

"But I can imagine all sorts of motives for all of them," Hugh said.

Doona grinned. "So can I."

"Let's start at the top of the list, then," John suggested. "Why might Mark have wanted Doug dead?"

"Maybe Mark's father preferred Doug to Mark," Hugh said. "Maybe he told his son that he was going to leave the bar to Doug instead."

"No one has said anything to suggest that Mark and his father didn't get along, though," Bessie argued.

"Maybe Mark was able to keep it a secret," Doona replied.

"Maybe Mark thought Doug was preventing him from accomplishing something," Hugh said. "Maybe Mark was interested in a woman who was in love with Doug. Or maybe Mark just wanted to try his hand at murder."

"Maybe Doug was having an affair with Mark's girlfriend," Doona suggested.

"Surely, that would have come up during the investigation," Bessie said.

"Not if they were really discreet," Hugh said. "Maybe Mark found out, but neither of them knew that he knew. Obviously, the girlfriend wasn't going to admit to it after Doug's death."

"But surely she must have suspected that Mark killed him, then," Bessie said.

"Maybe, but if she didn't think Mark knew about the relationship, she wouldn't have any reason to suspect him," Doona replied.

"Maybe Nolan needs to talk to Mark's former girlfriend again," Bessie said, making a note.

"Maybe he should look at the woman Mark started seeing next, too," Hugh said. "Maybe she was in love with Doug before he died."

"That might be a bit of a stretch," John said. "Which is not to say that Nolan shouldn't find out what he can about her."

"Are we done with Mark?" Bessie asked.

"I can't think of any other motives, but I still have Mark at the top of my list," Doona said.

Bessie nodded. "Andrew and I were talking about the possibility that Doug wasn't the intended victim."

Doona sighed. "Didn't we do enough of that with the last case?"

"We did a lot of it, which is probably why the idea came to me in the first place," Bessie admitted.

"Let's finish with motives for Doug's death first," John suggested. "Then we can talk about other possible scenarios."

"Anyone have any idea why Rusty might have wanted to kill Doug?" Hugh asked.

"They'd known one another for a long time," Bessie said. "Perhaps we need to know more about their shared history."

"There must have been disagreements over the years," John said. "Doug may not have even been aware that the man he thought was his friend was actually angry at him for something that had happened years earlier."

Bessie looked around the table. "If any of you were angry with me about anything, you'd tell me, right?"

Doona nodded. "Long before the resentment built up and I started planning how to kill you," she promised.

"It doesn't seem to be much of a motive," Bessie said. "But we don't have anything stronger."

"Why did Patti want to kill Doug?" Hugh asked.

Everyone exchanged glances.

"Maybe she had a thing for him and he didn't reciprocate," Hugh suggested.

"Or maybe he came on to her and didn't want to take no for an answer," Doona said.

"They were both single. I wonder why they weren't interested in one another," Bessie said. "Maybe Nolan could ask Patti about that."

"Are you curious why Doug and Tina weren't attracted to one another?" Hugh asked.

Bessie shook her head. "Everyone in the group knew that she was interested in Mark, including Mark. They all talked about it in their statements. Doug must have known as well."

"So what gives her a motive for killing Doug?" Hugh asked.

"I suppose Doug might have tried something anyway," Doona said. "Or maybe she changed her mind and set her sights on Doug, but he turned her down, too."

"The problem is, if any of these things had happened, surely the others in the group would have told the police about it," Bessie said. "No one mentioned any arguments between any of the campers."

"If I'd killed Doug, I think I would have told the police that he'd been fighting with everyone," Doona said.

"Except that would have been a red flag for the police

after everyone else said that no one was arguing the night of the murder," John said.

"I'd make a terrible killer," Doona said.

Everyone laughed.

"Do we want to talk about Bessie's theory, then?" Hugh asked.

"It isn't a theory," Bessie said quickly. "I just wondered, since there wasn't a clear motive for Doug's murder, whether someone else was meant to be the target."

"It's possible, of course, but it also complicates things," John said.

"I still don't understand how everyone slept through it all," Doona said. "They must have been drugged."

"Or just really tired after a day of hiking in the wilderness," Hugh said.

"Who wanted to kill Mark, then?" John asked.

"Everyone?" Hugh said questioningly.

"He didn't seem to have been very popular with the others," Bessie said. "Aside from Tina, of course."

"And maybe he turned her down, so she decided to kill him," Doona said. "Maybe she didn't realise that Mark had decided to stay with the other guys in their tent. Maybe she just assumed it was Mark in the third tent and stabbed him before she realised it was Doug."

"The killer either had a torch or used his or her hand to find Doug's chest," Hugh said. "He or she was too accurate at hitting the heart to have just been slashing around in the dark. I would argue that means that the intended victim was one of the men, even if it wasn't Doug."

John nodded. "The women were both significantly smaller than any of the men. The killer had to have been targeting one of the men."

"I don't think anyone had any reason to want Rusty dead,"

Doona said thoughtfully. "I will admit that my dislike for Mark may be a part of that, though."

"I think Nolan should keep the idea that Mark was the intended victim in the back of his mind when he questions the suspects again," Hugh said.

Bessie nodded. "It does seem as if the killer might have thought he or she was targeting Mark."

"I wonder what Mark would say if Nolan asked him who he thought wanted him dead," Doona said.

Bessie made a note. "I'll suggest that to Andrew," she said.

"I wonder if any of them still go camping together," Doona said. "I don't think they've ever been asked."

"It's an interesting question," John said.

Bessie nodded as she made another note. As she put her pen down, she yawned.

"It's getting late," John said after glancing at the clock. "We should wrap this up."

"I'm tired of talking about our campers, anyway," Doona said. "I can't help but feel as if one of them knows something."

"The killer knows a great deal," Hugh said.

Doona sighed. "Now we just need a confession."

"Before you all go," Bessie said. "I have one more little thing to discuss with you."

CHAPTER 10

"To do with the cold case?" Hugh asked.

Bessie shook her head. "To do with my cottage."

"You aren't thinking of selling it, are you?" Doona asked.

"Not even for a second," Bessie replied quickly.

"Sorry," Doona said.

"What about the cottage?" John asked.

"I've been wondering about the name," Bessie explained. "It already had the name Widow's Cottage when I bought it. I wanted to find out why."

"I hope it's an interesting story," Doona said.

"It might be very interesting," Bessie told her. "I haven't found out much yet, but I do know that I bought the cottage from Ewan and Margaret Christian. In turn, they bought the cottage from Margaret's sister, Joney Carlson. Joney was a widow."

"So there you are," Hugh said.

"Maybe. The cottage had its name when Ewan and Margaret bought it, but I'm still not certain that Joney was

THE MOSS FILE

the one who named it. I did find this, though." Bessie held up the copy of the newspaper's front page.

"A body on Laxey Beach!" Doona exclaimed. "I know it was some years ago, but I'm surprised I never heard about it."

"You're surprised?" John asked. "I thought I was familiar with every murder investigation that took place in Laxey for the last two hundred years. There weren't many, not up until a few years ago."

Bessie frowned. "I'd rather not think about how many murders happened in Laxey over the past three years or so. They seem to have stopped – for now, at least."

Hugh had picked up the paper when Bessie had put it down on the table. Now he looked up at Bessie. "It doesn't say that this man was murdered," he said. "It's possible that he simply had a heart attack while walking on the beach."

Bessie nodded. "And he may not have any connection to my cottage, either, but when Joney sold the cottage, the newspaper said that she'd been widowed almost exactly ten years before the sale. That headline is from almost exactly ten years before the sale."

"I can't give you access to the police files," John said. "But I can have a look and see what I can find. Records that are that old are housed in Douglas, in our archives, unless they're still active investigations."

"So if it was murder, the case was solved," Bessie said.

John nodded. "If it hadn't been solved, it would still be considered active, even after all these years."

"Andrew is having dinner with the Chief Constable tonight," Bessie told him. "He said he might see if the Chief Constable will let us take a look at the file."

John grinned. "I'll stay out of it for now, then. If the Chief Constable says no, my offer still stands."

"Thank you," Bessie said. "I should be able to find out

more from the Museum archives, but everything is on microfilm, and you have to book readers in advance."

"Depending on the outcome of the investigation, the file you want might be on microfilm in our archives," John said. "But if it is, it's easy enough to get copies made."

"We'll see what the Chief Constable says and go from there," Bessie said. "I just wanted to tell you all about it."

"I'm glad you did," Doona said. "I'd much rather think about that tonight than our cold case. The cold case is interesting, but your case is much closer to home."

"Quite literally," Bessie murmured.

Everyone agreed that Hugh should take the rest of the delicious Victoria sponge home to Grace. Bessie walked them all to the door and hugged them each in turn before they left. It was getting late, but there was no sign of Andrew's car. After pottering around the kitchen for several minutes, doing nothing, Bessie finally gave up and turned out the lights. Ten minutes later, she crawled into bed.

"Happy dreams," she told herself firmly.

~

WHEN SHE OPENED her eyes a few minutes past six the next morning, Bessie couldn't remember any of her dreams. "That works," she said softly as she got out of bed.

After getting ready for the day, she headed out for her walk. She was on her way back to Treoghe Bwaane when she spotted Andrew emerging from his cottage. She waved.

"Good morning," he said when she reached him.

"Good morning. I wasn't expecting to see you this early this morning. You were out quite late."

Andrew nodded. "The Chief Constable had a lot that he wanted to discuss, but I woke up at half six, wide awake and ready for the day."

"I hope you had a nice dinner, at least."

"It was very good, thank you."

"Ours wasn't." Bessie told Andrew about the less than wonderful food they'd eaten the previous night. "At least pudding was good," she concluded.

"And now, since you've been so patient and not asked, I shall tell you what the Chief Constable said about the police file from the body on the beach."

Bessie grinned. "I knew you'd get there eventually."

"He's going to have someone locate the file for him. Once he has it, he'll look it over and then decide whether we can have a look or not."

"I suppose that's better than nothing."

"I'm fairly certain that his taking a look before sharing it with us is just a formality. He's going to ring me in a day or two with an update."

"And tomorrow we can go back to the archives and see what we can find in the newspapers."

"Which means today we can focus on our cold case. Aside from the dreadful food, how was dinner last night?"

"We talked a lot, but we didn't get anywhere. We weren't really able to come up with any clear motive for anyone for murdering Doug. Then we talked about whether or not the killer thought he or she was killing someone else, but that just went in circles, really."

Andrew nodded. "I want Nolan to ask everyone about motives and also to suggest to each of them that maybe Doug wasn't the intended victim. It might be interesting to hear what they all think of that theory."

"If the killer did want to get rid of Doug, then he or she might be eager to support the idea," Bessie said thoughtfully.

"Maybe. We also have to consider that there wasn't any motive, that the killer struck for no reason."

Bessie sighed. "I hate that idea most of all. I know that it happens, but doesn't a killer who does that usually kill again?"

"Typically, yes, and none of the suspects in this case have ever been linked to any other suspicious deaths."

"Which doesn't prove anything, of course. Maybe he or she just got a lot smarter."

"I hope not. The last thing we want is killers getting smarter."

They'd slowly been strolling down the beach. Now Andrew stopped.

"I rushed outside when I saw you on the beach," he explained. "But I haven't had breakfast yet. I hope you don't mind if I turn around here."

"I'm more than happy to turn around. I already had my walk this morning."

"After I get breakfast, do you want to do something this morning?" Andrew asked when they reached his cottage.

Bessie thought for a minute and then shook her head. "I'm going to go back through the case file again. I want to try to get a better understanding of the sort of person Doug was."

"We haven't really talked that much about him, really. Maybe we should start there this afternoon. Shall we have lunch at the Seaview before the meeting?"

"Yes, please."

"I'll see you around midday, then."

As he went into his cottage, Bessie continued the short distance to hers. Inside, she made herself some tea and then sat down with her case file. As she read, she took notes every time anyone said anything about Doug. When she was finished, she frowned at her notes.

"Everyone says he was a nice person, but no one shared any stories about him. They say he was a good bartender, but was that what he wanted to do with the rest of his life?

Where would Doug be now if he hadn't been murdered twelve years ago?"

That question was still on her mind as she got ready to leave for lunch and the meeting. Andrew had a frown on his face when he arrived at Bessie's.

"What's wrong?" Bessie asked as soon as she'd opened the door.

"Is it that obvious?" he replied with a chuckle. "It isn't anything, really, just family problems."

"Do you need to stay here and deal with them before the meeting?"

"I wish it were going to be that easy, but these are things that will have to be dealt with when I return to London. It isn't anything terrible, just some bits and pieces that will take time and effort to resolve."

Bessie thought about asking more questions, but Andrew shook his head and smiled at her.

"So let's go and have a lovely lunch and talk about pleasant things," he said in a determined voice.

They chatted about holidays they'd taken over their lifetimes. Andrew had travelled a good deal more than Bessie, and she was happy to hear about his adventures in faraway places. The conversation continued over a delicious lunch. Andrew was still telling Bessie about a safari trip to Africa when they walked into the penthouse conference room just before two. Hugh was already there, sitting behind a plate filled with small squares of cake.

"There's going to be a big exhibition thing for brides in Douglas later this month," Hugh explained after they'd greeted him. "The pastry chef will be providing all kinds of different cake samples. Yesterday he started testing his recipes, which means he ended up with hundreds of small cubes of cake in dozens of varieties."

"And Jasper gave us trays and trays of them," Bessie said, smiling happily at the table near the back of the room.

Hugh nodded. "There are cards that identify each of the different cakes, fillings, and icings. Jasper wants us to rate our favourites."

"I know it's old-fashioned of me, but I still think a traditional wedding cake is best," Bessie said as she took a few squares of iced fruitcake.

"I don't think we had any other option when I got married," Andrew said. "I'm not certain how couples decide these days. Everything on the table looks delicious."

Bessie added a few of the other options to her plate and then got herself a cup of tea. Before she'd walked to the table, John and Doona arrived.

"Wedding cake samples?" John said, raising an eyebrow. "Is someone trying to tell me something?"

"Oh, hush," Doona said with a laugh.

By the time they'd filled plates and sat down, Harry and Charles had arrived as well. Once everyone was in place, Andrew cleared his throat.

"I hope you've all brought lots of questions for Nolan," he said.

"I want to know more about Mark's relationships with the others," Harry said. "Why was he there? Why was he friends with people that he seemed to consider beneath him?"

Charles nodded. "He's very successful now, but he still lives above that bar. Why?"

"We talked last night about whether Doug was the intended victim," Hugh said. "We agreed that the witnesses should be asked for their thoughts on that idea."

Andrew nodded. "It's an interesting idea."

"They need to be asked again who they thought killed

Doug," Harry said. "I want to see if anyone changes his or her answer."

"I think they should be asked what they think Doug would be doing now if he were still alive," Bessie said.

Everyone looked at her.

She shrugged. "No one really talked about Doug, not about who he was when he was alive. They all say they were his friends, but none of them seemed all that sad that he was gone. I want to hear what they say when they're forced to think about him."

"That's a good point," Andrew said.

"I think it might be useful for them to be asked about whether they think they were drugged that night or not," Harry said. "I still find it hard to believe that both Doug and his killer were wandering around camp in the dark and no one else woke up."

"If they were drugged, then Doug must have been the target," Doona said. "There was no evidence that he'd been drugged, was there?"

John flipped through his case file. "There were no drugs found in his system. He was drunk, but not drugged."

"Too bad they didn't test everyone at the campsite," Hugh said.

"I still want to know if the other friends that Patti mentioned had been invited to go camping or not," Bessie said. "And I want to know if the campers had been invited to the party that the other friends went to that evening."

Andrew nodded. "I have that one on my list already. Does anyone have any additional questions?"

"As always, it's frustrating not being able to question people ourselves," Hugh said.

"That's one of the downsides of being in a cold case unit," Andrew said. "Does anyone have anything they'd like to discuss about the case, based on the updated information you were given last time?"

Harry frowned. "I found Mark even less likeable than I found him in his earlier interviews. If he hadn't already been at the top of my list, he'd be there now."

"Did anyone find themselves rearranging their lists based on the updates?" Andrew asked.

A few people shook their heads. No one spoke for a moment.

"I thought I was going to move Patti up my list," Charles said eventually. "After what you said about her current husband, I thought she'd seem more likely, but in her most recent statement, she still managed to seem slightly naïve and sweet, even though she'd just married a much older and much wealthier man."

Harry nodded. "If I were Nolan, I'd be wary of her. I don't think she killed Doug, but I would be very suspicious if anything happened to her husband."

"Anything else?" Andrew asked.

"Do any of them still go camping?" Bessie asked, flushing as everyone looked at her.

"I'm not sure why that's relevant," Harry said.

"Maybe I'm just being nosy, but I think it might be interesting to know," Bessie replied. "I'm also curious which of the campers had camped together before. It was mentioned here and there in the statements, but I don't feel as if I have the complete picture. We know Rusty and Doug used to camp together a lot, but what about the others? Someone said that this had been the first time they'd gone camping in this particular group."

"I'll add those to the list. Anyone else?"

"Not really," Harry said. "I think we need answers to some of our questions before we can think about moving the case forward."

Andrew nodded. "I'll send the email as soon as I get back to my cottage. We may have some answers as soon as tomorrow, at least for some of the suspects. Nolan is hoping to speak to them all as quickly as possible."

"Are we meeting again tomorrow, then?" Harry asked.

"No, we'll give Nolan an extra day," Andrew replied. "If anything truly interesting comes back from Nolan between now and then, I can always arrange for an extra meeting."

Harry got to his feet. "I'll see you all the day after tomorrow, then," he said as he headed for the door.

Charles was right behind him. "I'll reread the file while we wait," he said on the way to the door.

As the door shut behind him, Hugh began filling a box with leftover cake squares. As Bessie and others followed suit, Jasper arrived.

"Knock, knock," he said as he stuck his head into the room. "I was just up here checking that housekeeping had done their usual excellent job in getting a few of the suites ready for guests when I saw people leaving from here. I hope that means I'm not interrupting anything important."

"We're finished with the meeting," Andrew assured him. "We're just packing up cake to take home."

"Excellent, but you all need to tell me which squares you enjoyed the most," Jasper replied.

He took notes while they each told him about their favourites.

"I very much enjoyed the traditional wedding cake," Bessie said when it was her turn.

Jasper nodded. "If it were up to me, that's all we'd offer for every wedding, but today's couples want options. In many cases, we end up providing two cakes, a traditional one to please the parents and then something else entirely for the happy couple."

He walked them all to the lift and then rode down to the ground floor with them.

"Thank you for the wonderful cakes," Hugh said as they emerged from the lift. "Grace is going to enjoy most of them, but Aalish will be allowed a few squares, too."

"I suppose I shall have to share mine with Helen," Andrew said.

John nodded. "And I'll share mine with Amy."

Bessie looked at Doona. "I'm going to eat all of mine myself," she said.

Doona laughed. "Me too."

Andrew drove them straight back to Laxey.

"With the time difference, Nolan might have time to start working through the suspects today," he told Bessie as he parked. "I'm eager to hear their answers to our questions and to get new updates on their lives."

Bessie nodded. "You go and send your email. I'm going to curl up with a good book."

"Dinner? We could go into Onchan. Maybe we should go and see what Dan is cooking today."

"Oh, that does sound good," Bessie said, thinking fondly of her friend who served small portions of multiple meals as the daily special in his restaurant.

"No doubt Helen will want to join us."

"Of course."

Andrew glanced at his watch. "Six or half six?"

Bessie shrugged. "Either will work for me. How long do you need to put together your email?"

He sighed. "Half six is probably better."

"I'll see you around half six, then."

Bessie went inside her cottage and locked the case file in a desk drawer. Then she curled up with a good book and let herself forget all about both the case and the history of her cottage for a short while.

CHAPTER 11

While Bessie enjoyed her book, she was ready to go to dinner at half six. She walked outside and found Andrew and Helen walking across the parking area.

"I'm so excited," Helen said as Bessie joined them at Andrew's car. "I love Dan's cooking so much."

"Did you get the email sent?" Bessie asked Andrew.

He nodded. "And I've already had a reply. All it said was that he had read through the questions and thought some of them were interesting and some of them were odd, but that he'd put them to everyone."

"Odd? I wish I knew which ones he thought were odd," Bessie said.

Andrew chuckled. "We're probably better off not knowing."

The drive to Onchan didn't seem to take long as the trio talked about some of the things they'd enjoyed at Dan's restaurant in the past.

"It looks busy," Andrew said as he pulled into the car park.

"Isn't it always?" Helen asked.

They walked into the building, stopping right inside the door. There was a short queue between them and the woman taking names. The man in front of them sighed deeply as the door shut behind Bessie.

"They should open a bigger restaurant," he grumbled.

"That would be nice," Andrew said.

"We could eat somewhere else," the woman with the man suggested.

He made a face. "The food here is worth the wait. I promise."

She shrugged. "It had better be. I'm starving."

When Andrew finally got to add his name to the waiting list, he was told that it would probably be a twenty-minute wait.

"That's fine," he assured the harassed-looking young woman.

The restaurant's foyer wasn't very large, and it was quite full of people. Bessie was starting to feel a bit claustrophobic when Carol spotted her.

"Bessie, hello," she called, waving as she rushed past. "So good of you to visit us again."

"You know I love Dan's cooking," Bessie replied.

Carol nodded and then kept going, delivering plates to a table near the back. A few minutes later, she returned to the foyer.

"How are you?" she asked, pulling Bessie into a hug.

"I'm very well. How are you?"

Carol shrugged. "I'm good. The baby is good, but not a baby any longer. Dan is good. The business is thriving, obviously."

Bessie looked around at the crowd. "Maybe it's time to look for a larger building."

"I feel as if we just moved in here, but you may be right.

Dan and I are talking about a lot of different options right now."

"Oh?"

Carol flushed. "Nothing I can talk about yet."

"You need a larger building," the man standing next to Bessie said.

"It's under consideration, but it isn't as easy as you'd think to move a restaurant," Carol explained. "And Dan already works far too many hours every week. A larger restaurant would mean even more work for him."

As a party of six were led away to an available table, a group of four walked into the building. Carol took a name from them and added them to the list.

"We'll let you get back to work," Bessie said when Carol walked back towards her. "But I want to see pictures of the baby when we have a table."

Carol nodded. "I have an entire album I can leave with you to go through at your leisure, but first I need to find you a table."

"You need to find me a table first," the man next to Bessie said. "I was here first."

Carol flushed. "Of course. I wasn't suggesting letting anyone skip the queue." She looked at Bessie. "Sorry."

"Not at all. We're happy to wait," Bessie said.

"What's Dan doing today?" someone in the crowd asked.

Carol grinned. "Our baby, Wendy, has been learning about shapes. Tonight's dinner and pudding plates are both celebrations of shapes."

A loud crashing noise interrupted Carol. She looked in the direction of the sound and then sighed.

"I need to go and help with that," she said. "Your waiter or waitress can tell you more."

Bessie, Helen, and Andrew entertained themselves while they waited for their table by coming up with different ideas for food in shapes. When they were finally seated, they all looked expectantly at their waiter.

"Today we celebrate shapes," he told them. "Each sample plate comes with a small serving of pasta stars in tomato sauce with a round meatball, a small square of filet steak with cubed potatoes, a triangle of chicken and leek pie, and an oval serving of steamed cod over seasoned rice."

"Oh, my goodness," Helen said. "Yes, please."

Bessie nodded. "But what about pudding?" she asked.

"One round chocolate chip cookie, one square of brownie, one star-shaped lemon tart, and one triangle of shortbread," he replied.

"I hope I can save room for all of that," Helen said.

"We can put pudding into takeaway containers for you," the waiter assured her.

They ordered drinks and they all ordered the sample plate. As soon as the waiter walked away, Carol came over and handed Bessie a small photo album. Bessie enjoyed looking through the pictures of little Wendy, who wasn't a baby any longer.

"She's adorable and she looks very bright," Bessie said as she handed the book back to Carol a few minutes later.

"She is very bright. We bring her here during lunch sometimes, and she's already eager to help. Of course, she's just in the way, but most of the customers seem to enjoy seeing her," Carol replied.

"I must come for lunch one day soon," Bessie said.

"Ring first to see if Wendy is here," Carol said. "My mother has her some days and, if it were up to her, she'd have her every day."

Bessie nodded. The pair chatted about Wendy for a bit longer before Carol had to rush away to deal with a large crowd that had just arrived without notice.

"I can't imagine running a restaurant business," Helen

said. "If I could cook like Dan, maybe I'd feel differently about it, but, as it is, it seems as if it's an awful lot of hard work."

"It does, indeed," Bessie replied as their waiter appeared with a tray full of plates.

He put a plate covered in food in front of each of them. "Does anyone need anything else right now?" he asked.

"It all looks wonderful," Bessie said, picking up her knife and fork.

"Indeed, thank you," Andrew added.

The man nodded and walked away.

Bessie took a bit of pasta and sighed happily.

"We should eat here every night," Helen said a short while later. "I don't think I'd ever get tired of Dan's cooking."

When they'd finished their meals, they all agreed to get their puddings boxed up to take with them.

"We'll walk for ten miles along the beach and then we'll enjoy them," Helen said.

"Ten miles?" Andrew echoed.

"Okay, maybe just five," Helen replied.

"I think a short stroll to Thie yn Traie and back is a better option," Andrew told her.

Helen laughed. "I was hoping that was five miles, at least in terms of calories burned."

"You will burn extra calories while walking on sand," Bessie told her.

They climbed into Andrew's car for the drive back to Laxey. When they got back to Bessie's, they put their boxes of pudding in Bessie's kitchen and then headed out for their stroll. It was cool and the sun had set some hours earlier, so Bessie gave them all torches to light their way.

"I'm too full to walk very fast," Helen said as they walked along the water's edge.

"We aren't in any hurry," Andrew said. "After this, we'll

have pudding, and then we can watch telly or read until bedtime."

"Except you'll want to check your emails," Helen said.

Andrew nodded. "But I'm not expecting anything interesting in them."

Bessie grinned. "Maybe you should check now, just in case there is anything interesting."

He shook his head. "I want to finish this walk and then eat my puddings. I'm sorry now that I didn't eat them at the restaurant."

A few minutes later, they reached the stairs to Thie yn Traie. As they turned around to walk back, Bessie saw something in the shadows further down the beach.

"Hello?" she called, wondering if Pat, the young man who looked after the holiday cottages, was out for a walk himself.

"Hello," a voice called back. "Aunt Bessie, is that you?"

The trio stopped. Bessie pointed her torch towards the approaching figure, smiling when she recognized Elizabeth Quayle.

"What are you doing down here after dark?" she asked the young woman when she joined them.

"I needed to get away for a few minutes, that's all."

"Is everything okay?"

Elizabeth shrugged. "Sometimes I just want to rewind time. I wish now that I'd talked my father out of that stupid holiday after the murder. If we'd stayed here, Mum could have been treated by doctors she knew and trusted. Dad could have kept working instead of taking time off and then deciding that he's quite happy at home, underfoot, all day long. And I could have kept my business going instead of having to try to build it all over again."

And you'd still be with Andy, Bessie added silently, guessing that Andy was the main thing on the young woman's mind.

"There's very little point in dwelling on the past," she said. "You can't change the choices you made before, but you can learn from them to hopefully make better choices in the future."

"I know, and I'm usually really good at not letting myself get dragged down by regrets. It's just been a difficult day, I think."

"Oh?"

Elizabeth sighed. "Dad and I spent the morning going over the plans for the house in Douglas. You know I want to transform it into a spa and an event centre. My father and I don't agree on anything to do with the transformation, though."

"I am sorry."

"Mum started sneezing after dinner. She insisted that it was just a tickle, but Dad is convinced that she's brewing something dreadful. She didn't want to ring the doctors. I get the feeling that she's becoming less and less happy with the team that looks after her here now."

"What a shame," Bessie said.

"I spent the afternoon trying to work with two of my brides – women for whom I'm planning weddings. One kept telling me that I was charging too much for my services, considering I'm rich already, and the other expected me to be able to use my connections – as if I have any connections – to get all manner of very famous people to attend her ceremony."

"Perhaps you should consider not working with either of them."

"Oh, I have." Elizabeth fell silent, her eyes on the sea.

"There's something else," Bessie said eventually.

"One of my friends saw Andy having lunch with a pretty blonde woman," Elizabeth said in a low voice.

"I see."

"She said they seemed very affectionate with one another, holding hands and whispering together."

"I think you need new friends."

Elizabeth chuckled. "I didn't want to hear it, but I do need to know if Andy is seeing someone else. It's better to learn about it from a friend than to see it for myself."

"There could be other explanations."

"There could."

"I can ring him and find out," Bessie offered.

"No, don't do that. It isn't any of my business, not any longer. We were good together and I thought – ah, but it doesn't matter what I thought. I was wrong. He moved on almost immediately and now he's done it again. That should tell me all that I need to know about the man, really, shouldn't it?"

"You're angry with him, even though he may just have been having lunch with a friend."

"I'm angry with myself for ever falling for him. I'm angry with myself for ending our relationship before I left the island. I'm angry with myself for not demanding that we talk as soon as I got back to the island. I'm angry with myself for not kissing him when we toured that stupid house in Lonan, when I had the chance. And I'm angry with myself for wanting to kiss him."

As tears streamed down Elizabeth's face, Bessie pulled her into a hug.

"You need to work out how you feel," she said. "If you still care for Andy and want to give your relationship another try, you need to let him know that before he ends up falling for someone else."

"I do still care for him, but I'm also still angry that he believed such horrible things about me. And I'm angry that he didn't kiss me when he had the chance, too."

Bessie chuckled. "That would have simplified things. Or maybe it would have just made you even angrier."

Elizabeth shrugged. "I can't even think about getting involved with anyone else. Every man I meet I compare to Andy, and they all come up short. I can't believe that he was engaged to someone else and then, when that didn't work out, that he's already found another woman. It just seems to prove that I was never all that important to him."

"Maybe he's just doing everything he can to try to forget how much he cares about you."

"I don't suppose it matters. For the longest time, I was worried about bumping into him somewhere on the island, but I hardly ever go anywhere, and he's probably busy in Lonan now anyway, working on his plans for his restaurant."

"I don't think the house sale is final," Bessie said.

"It will be soon, and as I understand it, the current owner has already given Andy a key and told him to come over whenever he wants to start measuring and planning."

"You know more than I do."

Elizabeth flushed. "I have friends all over the island, and they all seem to think that I want to hear about Andy all the time."

"Maybe it would be best if they stopped telling you what he's doing."

"Maybe."

"Are you going to be okay?"

She sighed. "Of course. I'm British. Stiff upper lip and all that. I just needed a walk on the beach to clear my head. Now I shall climb back up to the house and go to bed. Tomorrow I'm going to go back to Daddy's architect with my plans and make him redraw everything my way. If Mum is still sneezing, I'll ring her doctor and get someone to visit her. And then I'm going to ring some of my friends from across and invite them over for a weekend. They can all stay at the house in Douglas, and we can all go clubbing together. I'll have them bring a few single men with them. Maybe I'll meet someone special."

"Good luck with all of that."

Elizabeth grinned. "Thanks. Better days are coming. I'm going to make it happen."

Bessie, Helen, and Andrew watched as Elizabeth slowly climbed the many flights of stairs. When she reached the top, she waved to them with her torch and then disappeared from view.

"That poor child," Helen said.

Bessie nodded. "She's had a rough time lately. Maybe seeing some friends from across will do her some good. Before she started seeing Andy, she used to have friends come to visit a great deal."

"I feel sorry for any man she meets now, though," Helen said. "She's still rather desperately in love with Andy, isn't she?"

"She is, and I have to say that if Andy is seeing someone else, I'm a bit disappointed in him. I thought he was still in love with Elizabeth, too."

"He did get engaged to another woman while she was away," Andrew pointed out.

"Yes, but that woman pursued him and managed to convince him that Elizabeth had lied to him about some very important things. This is different."

"He's young and attractive and wealthy," Andrew said. "I suspect a lot of women are pursuing him all the time."

Bessie sighed. "And none of it is really my business. They are both good people, though, and I want them to be happy."

"Do you know what will make me happy?" Andrew asked.

"Pudding," both women said at the same time.

Andrew laughed. "Exactly."

Bessie opened the door to her cottage, and they went inside.

"The brownie is the best part," Helen said a short while later.

"I prefer the lemon tart," Andrew said.

"It's all good, but I think my shortbread is better," Bessie said with a grin.

"Your shortbread is better," Andrew agreed. "But that isn't to say this isn't delicious."

"I can't make shortbread to save my life," Helen said. "I've tried dozens of times and it never comes out right."

"I can give you my recipe," Bessie offered. "It's really very straightforward, and there are only a handful of ingredients."

"Mine just doesn't bake properly," Helen explained.

"You have to bake it slowly at a low temperature," Bessie told her. "But you don't have to bake it in a traditional circle. You can make smaller circles or even fancy shapes. Those bake much more quickly."

"Or I can just buy it in the shops," Helen said with a laugh. "It's been years since I tried to bake shortbread from scratch."

Bessie took another small bite of each thing on the plate. "The chocolate chip cookie is delicious. It reminds me of the cookies that my aunt used to bake at Christmas when I lived in America."

"They do lots of cookies for Christmas, don't they?" Helen asked.

"They do. Every family seems to have its own special recipes that get passed down through the generations. My sister always used to send me recipes that she was given by friends and by her husband's relatives."

"Did you try many of them?" Helen wondered.

"Years ago, I had little else to do besides bake. I used to

work out how to cut each recipe down until it would make only a dozen or so cookies, and then I'd save my pennies until I had enough money to buy all of the extra ingredients. Then I'd bake a batch or two of cookies and take notes on how they tasted."

"What fun," Helen said.

"It was fun, and it was part of the reason why I became so popular with the children of Laxey. Over the years, I acquired a great many recipes, and I began to bake more and more frequently. That meant that anyone visiting had a good chance of getting freshly baked cookies or biscuits or even cake."

Helen looked around the cosy kitchen. "Your cottage probably felt quite magical to some of the children."

Bessie nodded. "I never intended to become an honorary auntie to the village's children, but I didn't mind when I did."

After they finished their puddings, Andrew washed up their plates and teacups before he and Helen headed back to their cottage.

"If Nolan has had a confession, I want to hear about it immediately," Bessie told him.

"I'll ring you first," Andrew promised.

After they'd gone, Bessie sat down with the book she'd been reading before dinner. It was late, but she didn't think one extra chapter would hurt anything. Two hours later, she finished the book.

"It was just too good," she said as she got to her feet. "Besides, I couldn't leave the killer running around undetected. I had to make sure that he was caught."

She'd guessed the killer in the second chapter, and she'd been delighted to find that she was correct in the end. Her suspicions hadn't spoiled the story for her at all.

"And now I need sleep," she told her reflection as she combed her hair. "I'm quite late getting to bed, and tomorrow I'm going to the Museum to find out more about the man who was found dead on the beach outside."

She crawled into bed and fluffed her pillow.

"Straight to sleep," she ordered herself. "And no bad dreams."

CHAPTER 12

This time the instruction didn't seem to work. When Bessie opened her eyes the next morning just before six, she felt as if she'd done nothing but toss and turn in between bad dreams for the entire night.

"Coffee," she decided as she got out of bed.

She started the coffee maker and then went and showered and got dressed. When she got back downstairs, freshly brewed coffee was waiting for her.

"That's much better," she murmured as she sipped her first cup. After finishing two cups, she went out for her walk, striding briskly as she felt the caffeine fueling her system. Back at home again, she drank another cup while she cleaned the kitchen. Andrew knocked on her door at half nine.

"Ready for another session with the microfilm machine?" he asked.

Bessie made a face. "I should just take headache tablets now," she said.

The drive was uneventful. Andrew parked in the multi-storey car park and then they walked up to the Museum, arriving just as the doors opened for the day. Inside the library, Bessie found her microfilm waiting in the tray as promised. It only took her a few minutes to set up the film and scroll to the article that she'd printed on their last visit.

"I think I have this memorised," she told Andrew as she stopped on the front-page article.

He grinned. "So let's see what happened next."

Bessie scrolled to the next day. The main headline was about a fire that had taken place in Port St. Mary, but, at the bottom of the page, Bessie found the article she wanted.

"'Body on Beach Identified,'" she read.

Andrew looked over her shoulder as she quickly read the short article.

"So it was Joseph Carlson," Bessie said excitedly. "And they give his address by number and street, rather than by name."

"Which has to mean that Joney Carlson gave the cottage its name."

Bessie sat back with a small frown on her face.

"What's wrong?" Andrew asked.

She shrugged. "It just seems too simple. I suppose I thought I'd have to work a lot harder to find the information I wanted."

Andrew chuckled. "It's the historian in you. You aren't happy because you didn't have to do enough research."

"Which is silly of me. I should be delighted to have found what I wanted."

"Is that it, then?"

Bessie glanced at him. "Of course not. I still want to know what happened to Joseph."

"The article just says that the police are still investigating and that there will be an inquest in the future."

"It doesn't really sound as if it's a murder investigation, though," Bessie said. "Or maybe the newspaper was a bit more discreet about such things in those days."

"Let's see what else we can find," Andrew suggested.

Bessie scrolled forwards slowly. She couldn't find anything about the investigation in the paper from the next day. The day after that, she found a small article.

"'The inquest into the death of Joseph Carlson was adjourned to allow the police more time to investigate the incident,'" Bessie read.

"That isn't very helpful."

Bessie moved slowly through another month of newspapers, carefully reading every headline. "There isn't anything else," she said, sitting back and rubbing her eyes. "It's almost time to go, and my head is pounding, but I don't think we learned very much."

"We learned that the cottage didn't have its name when Joseph died," Andrew reminded her. "Which has to mean that Joney named it after his death."

"Yes, of course, but I still want to know what happened to poor Joseph."

"I'm sure we'll be able to find out more from the police file."

"If we get access to it."

"If the Chief Constable won't let us look at it, I'm sure he will answer questions about the contents."

"I hope so."

Bessie scrolled back and made copies of the two articles she'd found that mentioned Joseph. Then she rewound the film and put it back in its box. She and Andrew were on their way out of the room before the next person who'd booked their machine arrived.

"Thank you," Bessie said, handing the film to the woman behind the desk.

"Do you need to book another session?" the woman asked.

Bessie hesitated and then shook her head. "Not for today, anyway. We may be back."

"You know where to find us."

Bessie nodded, and then she and Andrew walked outside.

"Let's walk down to the promenade and enjoy seeing a different bit of the sea," Andrew suggested. "And then we can get lunch."

Bessie nodded. "That sounds good."

They walked silently for several minutes. Eventually Bessie sighed.

"What do you think happened to Joseph?" she asked.

Andrew shrugged. "Judging from the lack of interest in the story by the newspaper, I'm going to guess that he died of natural causes."

"Why was he alone on the beach? Did he go out for a walk the night before he was found, or did he go out very early that morning? Did his wife notice that he was missing? Was she worried? Was she thinking of going out looking for him before the police arrived? Did they have children? Was she too busy with them to worry about her husband?"

Andrew held up a hand. "I don't know the answer to any of those questions. Some of the answers will be in the police file, though. Having said that, I'm happy to speculate all afternoon if that's what you want to do."

Bessie chuckled. "Thank you. I'm sorry for throwing all those questions at you. It's odd, really, because until very recently I never gave any thought to the people who used to live in my cottage. Now I find I struggle to think of anything else."

"I've never wondered about the previous owners of any property I've owned. Of course, we moved a great deal. Perhaps if we'd stayed in one place and I'd come to love a property, I'd have cared more about its history."

"I never once wondered if children had ever lived at

Treoghe Bwaane," Bessie said. "And now I can't stop wondering if there used to be cots or small beds tucked into my spare bedrooms."

They'd reached the promenade. Andrew quickly took a seat on a nearby bench. Bessie sat down next to him and stared out at the sea.

"I want to know more about Joney," Bessie said. "I keep imagining that she was shocked and devastated when the police came and told her that her husband was dead. I can imagine her choosing to name the cottage in his honour."

"I used to live next door to a house that was named 'Seaside Cottage.'"

Bessie frowned. "When was that? I thought you'd always lived in London."

He chuckled. "I have always lived in London. Seaside Cottage was a small semi-detached house in the centre of a residential street, in a residential neighborhood in London. We were thirty-seven miles away from the closest beach."

"Why would anyone name their property Seaside Cottage if they were miles and miles from the beach?"

"I asked the owner that one day. He said his wife had given the house the name in honour of her father, who'd always said that one day he'd buy a house at the seaside. He'd passed away, having never managed to accomplish his dream. His daughter knew that she'd never be able to afford a house at the seaside, but when they bought their house, she did the next best thing and called it Seaside Cottage."

"Are you suggesting that Joney had some other reason for naming the cottage Treoghe Bwaane?"

Andrew laughed. "Not at all. I just thought it was an interesting story."

Bessie grinned. "It is interesting."

"But you're more interested in Joney."

"I am. I can't help but think of her as a rather tragic

figure. I've no idea how old she was when Joseph died, but I keep picturing her as a very young woman, perhaps because I lost Matthew when I was so young."

"Again, the police file should have that information."

"If we can't get access to the police file, I can look in the parish registers. I can probably find Joney there."

"How about some lunch?"

Bessie nodded and then slowly got to her feet. "I keep wondering why she sold the cottage," she said. "I wonder if she couldn't afford to stay there on her own."

"Maybe she got married again."

Bessie frowned. "I suppose that's possible, maybe even likely."

"But it doesn't fit with your image of her as a tragic heroine."

Bessie made a face. "I'm trying to keep an open mind about everything. I can't help it if my imagination runs away with itself sometimes."

Andrew nodded. "Here?" he asked as he stopped in front of one of Bessie's favourite restaurants.

"Yes, please," she said happily.

They were enjoying garlic bread and waiting for their meals before Bessie spoke again.

"I forgot to ask. Have you heard anything from Nolan?"

"I had an email waiting for me last night, but don't get excited. Nolan told me that he'd spoken to two of the four witnesses and that he'd asked them all of our questions and a few of his own. He promised to send full reports on those interviews and the other three by the end of today."

"So he didn't think he'd learned anything interesting," Bessie said.

"He didn't seem to think that anyone had said anything that moved the investigation forwards."

"Did he tell you which of the four he'd interviewed?"

Andrew shook his head. "I know he was going to be talking to Mark today. He told me that he'd had to book an appointment to see the man, but it could have been any of the others."

"I know we can't fly to Pennsylvania to question them ourselves, but that would be a good deal more satisfying."

"I agree, but that isn't how the unit works."

"Would Nolan be very upset if we just turned up?"

Andrew laughed. "I'm not certain how he'd feel, but I know my supervisor at Scotland Yard would be furious."

"Here we are," the waiter said, putting a plate of steaming spaghetti Bolognese in front of Bessie. He put Andrew's fettuccini Alfredo down and then smiled broadly. "Do you need anything else right now?"

"If I could have another drink, I'd appreciate it," Andrew replied.

"Right away."

Bessie picked up her fork and took a bite. "Wonderful, as always."

"What shall we talk about?" Andrew asked before his first bite.

"Why do people talk about angels dancing on the heads of pins? Where did that expression come from?"

Andrew frowned. "I've no idea."

The pair talked about other expressions and their likely or unlikely origins while they enjoyed lunch and pudding. Then they took a slow stroll along the promenade before returning to Andrew's car.

"Back to Laxey, or would you prefer to go somewhere else?"

Bessie chuckled. "Paris is supposed to be lovely this time of year."

"We can plan a trip to Paris for one day, but maybe not this afternoon."

"If we can't go to Paris or Pittsburgh, maybe we should just go back to Laxey."

As Andrew started the car, Bessie had a thought. "Or we could visit a friend of mine," she said.

Andrew looked at her. "Do you want to go and visit a friend?"

She hesitated and then nodded. "She isn't really a friend, more of an acquaintance. Harriet lived in Laxey for most of her life, but she's now living in a care home here in Douglas."

"Should I ask why you suddenly want to visit Harriet?"

"When she lived in Laxey, she didn't live far from the beach. And she's nearly a hundred. She's the only person I can think of who might have known Joney Carlson."

"In that case, where am I going?"

Bessie gave him directions to the large care home facility on the outskirts of Douglas. He parked in a visitor spot, and then the pair made their way inside.

"How can we help you?" the receptionist asked as they approached the desk that took up most of the small lobby.

"I was hoping to visit Harriet Caine," Bessie told her.

"Ah, Mrs. Caine loves visitors," the woman replied. "Do you visit her often?"

Bessie flushed. "I haven't been to see her since she moved here. I used to know her when she lived in Laxey."

The woman raised an eyebrow. "Mrs. Caine has been here for four years now. I'm afraid you might find that she's changed somewhat from when you last saw her."

"Does she have problems with her memory?" Bessie asked.

"She has good days and bad days," the woman told her. "She's nearly a hundred years old, so that's to be expected, of course."

"Yes, of course."

"Even if she doesn't remember you, she'll be delighted to see you. As I said, she loves having visitors."

Bessie nodded. The woman pushed a button on the desk. A moment later, the door behind her opened.

"Ah, Aunt Bessie, hello," the woman who walked out from behind the door said.

"Annabella Cross, I didn't know you were back on the island," Bessie exclaimed.

The woman shrugged. "I was in Liverpool for twenty-five years, but when I finally gave up on my marriage, I decided to come back here. We lost Dad a few years ago, but Mum is living here and loves it. Every time I came to visit, I thought I'd be a lot happier working here than I was in the place I worked in Liverpool."

"And are you?"

"Oh, goodness, yes," Annabella laughed. "I bought a flat nearby, so I can walk to work, and I can see Mum every day. Moving back was the best decision I ever made."

"I'm glad to hear that."

"But what brings you here?"

"I want to have a quick chat with Harriet Caine."

Annabella made a face. "Good luck with that," she said, before laughing. "The problem will be making it quick, that's all. Mrs. Caine can talk for England. I wouldn't mind so much, but none of her stories are very interesting."

Bessie chuckled. "I'm hoping she might remember one of the former owners of my cottage."

"You can ask her, but I wouldn't put a lot of faith in what she says. She told me a long story the other day about how her children used to sail back and forth to England in a bathtub."

"Oh dear," Bessie said.

"But come and have a chat with her, by all means. She'll be delighted to see you."

Annabella led Bessie and Andrew down a short corridor before turning down a longer one. About halfway along that hallway, she stopped and knocked on a door.

"Ah, Mrs. Caine, you have visitors," Annabella said loudly as she pushed the door open.

Bessie smiled at the woman who was sitting in a chair near the window. She looked older than Bessie remembered, but she was smiling as Bessie and Andrew walked into the room.

"I know you," Harriet said. "I just can't quite remember your name."

"I'm Bessie Cubbon, and this is my friend Andrew Cheatham."

Harriet frowned. "We were neighbours."

Bessie nodded. "I own Treoghe Bwaane, a cottage on Laxey Beach."

Harriet stared past her with a small smile on her face. "I always wanted to live right on the beach, but I never got the chance. I did love our little house above the beach, though. I could see the water from some of the windows."

"Do you remember my cottage?" Bessie asked. "It's the very first one on the beach as you come down the hill."

"Yes, of course. It's very small. It never would have worked for us. I had six children, didn't I?" She looked at Annabella, who nodded.

"They come to visit sometimes. Horace was just here last week," Harriet said.

Bessie frowned. Horace had been Harriet's oldest son. She remembered how devastated the woman had been when Horace had been killed in a car crash when he was in his mid-twenties.

"Mrs. Caine gets visitors all the time," Annabella said.

Harriet nodded. "All of my children and grandchildren

come to see me. My husband, though, he doesn't visit very often. I suppose he's busy with work."

Bessie knew that Harriet's husband had passed away more than thirty years earlier. "Do you remember the couple who owned my cottage before me?" she asked.

Harriet stared at her. "What cottage is that?"

"Treoghe Bwaane," Bessie replied. "I bought it from Ewan and Margaret Christian."

"Ah, I remember Margaret," Harriet said. "She was a thoroughly unpleasant person."

"Was she?"

"She didn't want to live in Laxey. She wanted to live in Paris."

"Why did they buy a cottage in Laxey, then?"

"Because they couldn't afford Paris, of course." Harriet sighed. "I went to Paris once. It was lovely."

As Harriet told a very long and boring story about wandering around the streets of Paris with her husband, Bessie looked at Andrew. He shrugged.

"Is that why they sold the cottage to me, then?" Bessie asked when Harriet paused for a breath. "Did they move to Paris?"

"Did who move to Paris, dear?" Harriet asked.

"Ewan and Margaret Christian."

"I'm afraid I don't know them. Do they live near here?"

Bessie shook her head. "Do you remember Joney Carlson?" she asked a bit desperately.

Harriet frowned. "She lost her husband. He died on the beach."

"Yes, that's right."

"She was very young when it happened. Or maybe I was very young when it happened. I don't really recall."

"Do you remember anything else about her husband, Joseph?"

"He was busy with work. Men were in those days. They didn't sit around and share skeet with one another the way that the women did."

As Harriet launched into another long story, Bessie glanced at her watch. Eleven minutes later, she'd finally had enough.

"Harriet, I'm sorry to interrupt, but my friend and I have an engagement elsewhere. It's been lovely to see you again," she said.

Harriet nodded. "It's been lovely to see you, too, Betty. Tell your son, Winston, that I was asking about him."

"Yes, of course," Bessie said.

"I'll show you out," Annabella said.

Bessie and Andrew followed her back to the foyer.

"She gets confused a great deal," Annabella said to Bessie.

"Yes, but she was right about Joney's husband," Bessie replied. "He did die on Laxey Beach."

"My goodness, how dreadful."

"Thank you for letting us see Harriet."

"Oh, you're very welcome. As I said, she loves having visitors."

"Do her children visit often?"

"One daughter comes to see her every day. The others come less frequently, but they do visit. She has seven grandchildren, but they usually only visit on Christmas and on Mrs. Caine's birthday."

Bessie nodded. "Of course, two of her children have passed away."

Annabella grinned. "But Mrs. Caine reckons they visit quite often, anyway."

"Maybe they do," Bessie said.

"It wouldn't surprise me," Annabella told her. "My ex-husband haunts me and he's still alive."

Bessie laughed and then said her goodbyes, thanking the

woman again. Then she and Andrew headed back out to his car.

"I'm sorry to have wasted your time," Bessie said as Andrew began to drive away from the building.

"It wasn't a waste of time. Harriet was charming."

Bessie laughed. "Her stories were both long and boring."

"Yes, but she's nearly a hundred years old. She's entitled to tell long and boring stories."

"I wish she would have remembered more. She knew them all."

"Perhaps, if you visit her again one day, she'll remember more."

"Perhaps one day when I have more time to spare."

"Indeed."

"I thought I might just read a book with what is left of the afternoon," Andrew said as he parked next to Bessie's cottage.

"We can't do much about the cold case until we hear back from Nolan. You may as well enjoy a book."

"And what will you be doing?"

Bessie laughed. "The same thing, I think."

"You're welcome to come and read in my cottage."

Bessie made a face. "Your furniture isn't terribly comfortable. Why don't you come and read in my cottage instead?"

The pair enjoyed a quiet afternoon in Bessie's cottage. Helen joined them for dinner at the local pub, and then Bessie curled up with her latest book and read again until it was time for bed.

"Tomorrow we get answers to some of our questions," she told her reflection as she put toothpaste on her toothbrush. "I just hope there is something in them that helps us move the case forward. Otherwise, we might be stuck."

CHAPTER 13

Bessie spent a quiet morning at home, only being interrupted once when Andrew came over for a quick cuppa.

"I don't want to go too far from my laptop this morning," he told Bessie as she prepared the tea. "Nolan is sending statements, one after the next, and I'm trying to read through them so that we can talk productively about the answers to our questions."

"You are going to give us all copies of the statements, aren't you?"

He nodded. "Jasper will let me print them on a printer at the Seaview. I've done it in the past."

"Did Nolan manage to speak to everyone, then?"

"He did, and some of the answers I've read so far have been quite interesting."

Bessie made a face. "And you won't share them with me now."

"I'd rather wait for the meeting."

"Do you think anyone said anything that might help us solve the case?"

He shrugged. "Nothing has jumped out at me as being useful, but that's why we have an entire unit of people working on the case. It's entirely possible that I missed something."

"I thought this one would be easier than it's proving to be."

"Indeed. When I read the initial report, it seemed considerably less complex than our last case. It isn't any easier, though."

"We solved the last one. We can solve this one."

"I hope so."

After Andrew left, Bessie grabbed a biography of Anne of Cleves from her bookshelf and enjoyed spending some time reading about the woman she considered Henry the Eighth's luckiest wife.

"She certainly had the happiest ending," Bessie murmured as she put the book down to make herself some lunch.

After lunch, she read for a bit longer before getting ready to go out. Andrew knocked on her door at half one.

"Ready?" he asked.

"Yes, and eager to hear what you've learned."

"I'm eager to share it. I've told Nolan we'll be back with more questions later today."

"Maybe the right questions to get the case solved."

They talked about Anne of Cleves on the drive. When they arrived at the Seaview, Andrew asked Sandra if he could use a printer. She quickly helped him print the pages of each of the recent interviews and then made copies for him for each of the unit members. Bessie waited in the lobby, watching the people going in and out, and imagining where they were all going and why.

"We're in the penthouse again," Andrew told her when he rejoined her. "Today we have rather more ordinary biscuits, or so I'm told."

In the conference room, Bessie selected a few biscuits from the table at the back and then poured herself a cup of tea. Andrew did the same. They were talking about Catherine Howard, Henry's fifth wife, when Hugh and Doona arrived together.

"Good afternoon," Bessie said.

"Hello," Doona said. "John had a meeting here in Ramsey, so I drove myself today," she explained.

"And I was very nearly late," John added, as he walked in while Doona was talking. "The meeting ran over, as they nearly always do."

"Ours rarely do," Andrew said.

John nodded. "You are very good about getting through the business at hand and ending the meeting on time. Not everyone who runs meetings has those skills."

Harry and Charles arrived a minute later. After everyone was seated, Andrew began.

"I've read through all of the interviews that Nolan conducted over the past two days. Then I tried to compile everyone's answers to the various questions that we put forward. I won't promise to have done a perfect job, but I did my best. I'm going to share how everyone answered each of our questions, and then we can talk about the various replies. I'm going to do this in no particular order, because I didn't see anything in any of the answers that I think moves the case forwards."

"That's disappointing," Hugh said.

"I'm hoping that together we'll be able to pull some additional questions from the answers," Andrew said.

Bessie picked up her pen, ready to take notes.

"I want to start with the question of whether they were drugged or not," Andrew said. "First, I'll share with you that Nolan told me that he thought it was unlikely. He said that the campgrounds were searched and that nothing was found that suggested that anyone had brought any drugs to the camp. The campers were all also searched, and they left their belongings behind. Of course, it's possible that the killer had a small bottle of something in a pocket and then simply threw the bottle into the woods before the body was found, but, according to Nolan, the search stretched out in every direction at least as far as someone could throw a bottle."

"The bottle might have been buried," Hugh suggested.

"Nolan also stated that no one acted as if they'd been drugged. He believes they were just drunk and tired and simply slept soundly."

"And what did the suspects say?" Harry asked.

"Mark said that he was certain he hadn't been given anything," Andrew told him. "He admitted that he'd had six beers and said that was enough to knock him out until morning, especially after all the hiking they'd done to get to the campsite."

"Would the killer be more or less likely to want the police to think they were drugged?" Hugh asked.

Everyone exchanged glances.

"I think that probably depends on whether they actually were drugged or not," John said eventually.

Hugh chuckled. "So we're no further along, really."

"What did everyone else say?" Harry asked Andrew.

"Rusty said anything was possible, but that he didn't remember feeling off the next morning. Then he said that trying to remember how he'd felt on a random day twelve years earlier was impossible."

"I'd have expected all of them to have rather vivid memories from that particular day," Harry said. "It wasn't random at all."

Andrew nodded. "Patti said that she didn't think she'd been drugged, either, but that she did remember sleeping very soundly. Tina was the only one who seemed to give the idea serious consideration. She told Nolan that it was possible, maybe even likely, because she couldn't imagine how they'd all slept through the murder."

"Which is why we asked the question in the first place," Charles said.

"Bessie was curious about the other three friends," Andrew continued. "They were all together at a party, and she wondered whether they'd been invited to go camping and also whether the campers had been invited to the party."

"Is Nolan going to interview the other three friends, too?" Doona asked.

"He will if we think it's relevant. Let me tell you what the others said in answer to that question, though. Mark told Nolan that he barely knew the other three people, and that he didn't know the person who was having the party at all. He said if he hadn't gone camping that weekend, he would have spent the weekend at the bar."

"Not with his girlfriend in Florida," Hugh said.

"Evidently not," Andrew said. "Rusty said that he really didn't remember, but that he'd probably been invited to the party. He said that back in those days he would have just about always picked a camping trip over a party in the city. As for whether the others had been invited on the camping trip, he said he wasn't certain but that he didn't think any of them would have been interested in coming along. Patti said much the same thing. She was certain she'd been invited to the party but said that she preferred a camping weekend to getting drunk in someone's flat and then having to get a bus home. She also said that the other three friends weren't really interested in camping."

"And what did Tina have to say?" Doona asked.

"That she didn't remember anything about any party and that she barely knew the other people that Nolan named," Andrew said.

"It seems as if she was very much on the periphery of the group," Harry said.

Andrew nodded. "Someone asked about the groups that had gone together in the past. We know Rusty and Doug camped together fairly often. Patti sometimes joined them, but, when she did, they always camped in a designated area with a few of Patti's other friends. This trip was the first time that Mark had ever gone camping with any of them. He usually went with some people he knew from work. They typically stayed in a cabin just inside the Forest. Mark admitted that this trip was his first time staying in a tent."

"Interesting," Harry said. "What made him suddenly decide he wanted to camp in a tent with a bunch of people who weren't really his friends?"

"Nolan asked him that question. According to Mark, he was trying to get to know Doug better because he was already thinking ahead to when he'd be taking over the bar. He said he thought Doug was good at his job, and he was hoping to convince Doug to take classes in business management at night so that he could eventually promote him to manager at the bar."

"But at that point, Mark was working for a bank and his father was in good health," Hugh said.

Andrew nodded. "I can only tell you what Mark told Nolan."

"What about Tina? Had she been camping with any of the others before?" Bessie asked.

Andrew shook his head. "Everyone agreed that Tina had never gone with any of them before. Tina told Nolan that she had never given the matter much thought but that she was certain she'd been camping with most of the others at least a few times before the murder."

"What an interesting lie to tell," Charles said.

"Why would she lie about that?" Bessie wondered.

"Maybe to make her presence on this trip feel less out of the ordinary," Harry suggested. "Maybe to hide the fact that she'd only gone on this trip because she wanted to murder someone."

"More likely to hide the fact that she only went on this trip because she wanted to get closer to Mark," Doona said.

Harry shrugged. "Either way, she appears to have lied to Nolan."

"When Nolan pushed her a bit harder, she admitted that she hadn't actually done all that much camping as an adult. She told Nolan about some trips she'd taken with her parents as a child but couldn't actually give him any details about any trips she'd taken after the age of eighteen."

"So she lied to the police and to her friends in order to be included in the trip," Bessie said. "The question is, did she do it to get closer to Mark or to kill Doug?"

"Maybe she was hoping to kill Mark," Doona said.

"Nolan also asked all of them if they still go camping. None of them have been on a camping trip since the murder, although Rusty did tell Nolan that he and his son sometimes sleep outside in a small tent in their back garden."

"I don't think I'd ever want to camp again, either," Doona said.

"We talked a bit about Mark and his relationships with the others," Andrew said. "Harry wanted that pinned down a bit more. When Nolan asked Mark about each of the others, Mark said that he'd liked and respected Doug, and that he thought Rusty was okay. He said he never would have gone camping with them if he hadn't thought they were okay. He also said he thought Patti was sweet but not his type. As for Tina, he said he barely knew her and had never been interested in getting to know her any better."

"Did he know that she was interested in him?" Doona asked.

"When asked, he admitted that Doug had told him that Tina was interested, but that he'd immediately told Doug that he was definitely not interested in her. He said Doug told him that he'd try to let Tina down gently."

"When was this?" Harry asked.

"In the afternoon, while they were hiking in the woods," Andrew replied.

"What if Doug asked Tina to meet him for a chat after the others were in bed?" Doona asked. "Maybe, when Tina heard what he had to say, she was so angry that she killed him."

"I hope Nolan asked Tina about the conversation," Bessie said.

"He did, but let me go back a bit and talk about how the others felt about Mark. I'll get to Tina in a second. Rusty said that he didn't know Mark well, but he knew that Mark could get Doug fired if he wanted to, so he was always willing to invite Mark along when he and Doug were making plans. He said he didn't really care for Mark, but he didn't dislike him, either. Patti said that she found him a bit intimidating because he was so much wealthier than any of them, but that he'd always been polite to her whenever they'd spoken. She also said that the tents that he'd supplied were much nicer than anything she'd ever seen before and that he hadn't had to get three of them. He could have just brought one for his own use."

"He said he'd brought three because he didn't want to be the only one in a tent, right?" Hugh asked.

Andrew nodded. "That's what he said at the time, anyway. It might be helpful to ask him again, though."

"It might be interesting to hear his response," Harry said. " But you were going to tell us what Tina said about Mark."

Andrew grinned. "She said that they'd been flirting with one another for months, but that it hadn't gone any further because her divorce hadn't been final. She also said that she believed that Mark brought an extra tent so that they would have a place to be alone together. She said that if they'd gone out on Friday, as originally planned, she knew they'd have shared the tent on Saturday night."

"And what about the conversation that Mark said he had with Doug?" Hugh asked.

"According to Tina, Doug never said anything to her about Mark."

"Did Mark seem to think that Doug had spoken to Tina?" Bessie asked.

"He wasn't certain. He said that Doug and Tina had spent some time talking together after his conversation with Doug, but he doesn't know what they discussed. Tina said they talked about the weather and edible mushrooms."

Bessie sighed. "I'm not certain we're getting anywhere."

"Mark was also asked why he still lives above the bar," Andrew continued. "He told Nolan that he felt connected to his father there. He said they'd had a difficult relationship over the years, but that he missed the man and that he couldn't imagine living anywhere else."

"Nolan also asked them all whether they'd ever considered that Doug may not have been the intended victim," Andrew said. "That brought some interesting replies."

Bessie took her last sip of tea and then frowned. She wanted more, but she didn't want to interrupt Andrew.

"Mark said that he'd always wondered why anyone would kill Doug, who was just an ordinary person. He suggested again that the killer was someone from outside the campsite who'd simply wanted to see what it felt like to kill someone. When Nolan suggested that the killer might have thought he or she was killing him, apparently Mark went pale and quiet."

"So he'd never given that idea any thought," Harry said.

"Apparently not, but, once he did, he had a lot to say. He

basically told Nolan that all of the others had motives for killing him."

"We thought the same," Bessie said.

Andrew nodded. "Nolan said that he thought that Mark was still somewhat shaken by the idea by the time they finished speaking."

"I'd be frightened if I thought someone had stabbed a man to death, thinking it was me," Hugh said.

"What did the others think of the idea?" Harry asked.

"Rusty said the only person anyone might have wanted dead out there was Mark, so maybe he should have been the victim. But he also said that he didn't see how anyone could have made that big of a mistake. He said that Mark and Doug had very different body types and that it should have been obvious that it was Doug in the third tent."

"Rusty didn't think the killer might have wanted to target him?" Hugh asked.

"Not at all. Rusty insisted that no one at the camp had any reason to want him dead. He said the same about Doug, though."

Bessie sighed. "What about the women?" she asked.

"Patti found the idea that someone else might have been the target worrying. She said that it was bad enough that someone had murdered one of her friends. If the killer had been trying to target someone else, he or she might try again one day."

"She isn't wrong," Harry said. "Have there been any attempts on the lives of any of the suspects since the murder?"

"I'd like to think that, if there had been, the suspect would have reported it to the police," Andrew said. "But I'll have Nolan ask them all to be certain."

"What did Tina say about the possibility that Doug wasn't the killer's target?" John asked.

"She said that she'd never understood why anyone killed Doug, but that she could have understood it if Mark had been the victim. Of course, she insisted that she didn't have a motive for killing Mark, but she said that Rusty definitely did."

"What motive?" Doona asked.

"She told Nolan that Rusty had frequently complained to her about Doug's friendship with Mark. She reckoned that Rusty was jealous of Mark's success and of how close Mark and Doug were."

"And did Rusty admit to the same?" Bessie asked.

"Nolan talked to Tina after he'd already spoken to Rusty. He's going to ask him about that matter when he goes back with our next set of questions."

"Fair enough," Harry said.

"They were all asked again who they thought killed Doug," Andrew said. "With the idea in their heads that the killer might have been targeting someone else, Nolan got some different answers this time. For a start, Rusty suggested that Tina might have been upset enough to want to kill Mark and drunk enough to stab the wrong man."

"Even though he'd just argued that the two men had very different body types," Bessie said.

Andrew shrugged. "Mark said he thought any of them might have done it, but he seemed to think that Rusty was jealous of his friendship with Doug and that Tina was angry at being rejected."

"If Patti did it, we'll all be shocked," Bessie said.

"What did she say this time when Nolan asked her who she thought did it?"

"She said that she could imagine Tina being upset enough at Mark to stab him, but she said she thought that if Tina had done it, she probably hadn't meant to kill him."

"So she still didn't want to accuse a friend directly," Charles said.

"And we've already talked about what Tina said," Doona said.

Andrew nodded. "She told Nolan that the killer had to have been Rusty, if Mark was the target, and she said that the whole thing finally made sense to her now."

Bessie frowned. "And she thought Rusty wanted to kill Mark because Mark was getting too close to Doug?"

Andrew nodded. "That's what she said."

"I think Nolan needs to take a good look at Tina," Harry said.

Bessie nodded. "Maybe he needs to find out more about Tina's relationship with Doug."

Andrew made a note. "The last thing that Nolan asked them was Bessie's question about what they thought Doug would be doing now if he were still alive. Nolan added to it, also asking what they thought they would be doing if Doug were still alive."

"That makes sense," John said.

"And before we talk about that, I need more tea," Andrew announced.

Everyone got up and got themselves more to eat and drink. Even Harry got himself a cup of coffee. Bessie sat down and took a sip of tea before she picked up her pen, ready to take more notes.

CHAPTER 14

"Where should I start?" Andrew asked as he flipped through his notes.

"Mark," Doona and Charles said together.

Andrew chuckled. "We always start with Mark, don't we? Right, Mark said that if Doug were still alive, he'd probably be managing the bar, and maybe some of Mark's other properties as well. When asked what he'd be doing, he said that Doug's death hadn't changed his life, not as significantly as his father's death, anyway. That was the death that put him on the path he's currently following. He added that he has no regrets about leaving banking and taking over the business, but he does wish that he had a reliable manager to run things on his behalf."

"So he hasn't found anyone to replace Doug?" Harry asked. "It's been twelve years."

"He told Nolan that he's worked with probably a dozen different bartenders since Doug died and none of them have been smart enough to be promoted to manager. He said he keeps trying to find the right person, but most people who want to tend bar for a living don't want to go back to school and move into management. He admitted that he wasn't certain that Doug wanted to do that, either, but at least he'd been planning to suggest it to Doug."

"I'm shocked that he didn't feel that Doug's death changed his life," Doona said. "The man was murdered just a few feet away from where he was sleeping."

"Has anything changed in his life over the past year?" Hugh asked.

Andrew shook his head. "He has a different girlfriend. He's only been seeing this one for a few months, and he told Nolan that he was probably going to end things soon. He just didn't feel that things were working well between them."

"I wonder how she feels," Bessie muttered.

"Let's talk about Rusty," Andrew said. "Nolan said Rusty looked shocked when he was asked about where Doug would be now. Then he laughed and said that he supposed that Doug would be in the exact same place he'd been twelve years earlier. He reckoned that he and Doug would both still be working their respective jobs, drinking too much, and trying to find women who were attracted to them in spite of their jobs and their drinking habits."

"So he changed his life because of the murder," Charles said.

Andrew nodded. "He told Nolan that Doug's death had been a real wake-up call for him. At twenty-six, he'd felt as if he were going to live forever and could do anything with his life. After Doug died, he realised that every day was precious and that he was wasting his life."

"So he benefitted from Doug's death, however indirectly," Harry said.

"Did Doug leave a will behind?" Hugh asked.

Andrew shook his head. "It's in the file somewhere. He didn't have a will, but he also didn't have anything to leave to anyone. His parents cleared out his flat. According to Nolan, he had less than two hundred dollars in his bank account when he died. The bar owed him some back wages, but he didn't have any life insurance or anything like that."

"I didn't think he'd been killed for his money, but I did wonder," Hugh said.

"Has Rusty made any big changes to his life in the past year?" Charles asked.

"His wife is expecting another baby any day now," Andrew told them. "Apparently it's a little girl this time. Nolan said Rusty is very excited."

Bessie made a note and then looked up at Andrew. "What about Patti? What did she think Doug would be doing now?"

"Patti said she didn't think he'd have changed much. She said he was very happy with his life just the way it was, so why would he change anything? She also said that she hoped he'd have found himself a girlfriend, because he occasionally commented that a girlfriend was the only thing missing from his life, but she reckoned that he'd have been happy enough on his own."

"And what did she think that she would be doing if Doug were still alive?" Doona asked.

"She said she didn't change her life because of Doug's death. She said she'd always planned to do great things and that she would probably be in the exact same place, regardless. She'd just have her friend Doug around sometimes."

"And she's still married to her old and rich husband?" Harry asked.

Andrew nodded. "They went on a cruise for their first wedding anniversary. Patti showed Nolan pictures of the pair of them on excursions every time the ship docked. She's pushing him in a wheelchair, but he looked as if he was having a wonderful time."

"How did she look?" Harry asked.

"Nolan said she looked blissfully happy in every picture."

"Maybe they truly are in love," Doona said.

"Or maybe she just spends all of her time thinking about her future inheritance," Harry said.

"That just leaves Tina," Bessie said.

"Yes, and Tina's response was the one that Nolan found the most interesting. When he asked Tina where she thought Doug would be today if he hadn't been killed, she said married with children."

"Wow, that is interesting," Hugh said. "No one else seemed to think that he was interested in either."

"When Nolan asked why she thought that, she said because that was what men did once they hit thirty. Before that, they played hard, breaking hearts as often as they could, and then, when they hit thirty, they found a willing woman and got married and had babies."

"Is it just me, or does she sound bitter?" Doona asked.

"She always sounds bitter," Hugh said with a laugh.

"Yes, but she doesn't usually direct her bitterness towards Doug. Is it possible there was something there?" Bessie asked.

"Everyone talked about how she was interested in Mark," Andrew said.

"Maybe she was just pretending to be interested in Mark," Bessie said thoughtfully. "Maybe she was trying to make Doug jealous."

"There's a lot of speculation there, but it's interesting speculation," Harry said.

"What did she say about what she'd be doing if Doug were still alive?" Doona asked.

"She said she'd probably be married with brats at home, too."

"Yikes," Doona said. "I think it's a good thing she never had kids."

"I assume she said she'd be married to Mark," John said.

Andrew shook his head. "Actually, she didn't. She just said that she thought she'd be married with children. As it is, she's still working in the same café and still living in the same flat as a year ago."

"Nolan should have asked them all what they thought the others would be doing if Doug were still alive," Bessie said.

"He did ask Tina that. She just laughed and said that she reckoned Doug's death hadn't done much to upset any of the others. She said they were all exactly where they would have been, regardless."

Bessie drank the rest of her tea while she tried to think. The others were all similarly silent. Eventually Harry spoke.

"There isn't anything obvious in any of that, but my gut feeling is that Tina needs to be questioned again."

Andrew nodded. "I agree."

"She needs to be asked about her relationship with Doug," Harry said. "We're probably grasping at straws, but I feel as if there might have been something there, something she didn't want anyone to know about then and something she really doesn't want anyone to know about now."

"Nolan should ask the others about Tina and Doug," Bessie said. "I know they were all asked about all of the different relationships in the past, but this time they need to be asked very specifically about Tina and Doug. Is there any chance the pair were seeing one another in secret? Is it possible that Tina was interested in Doug but he wasn't aware of her interest? Is it possible that Doug was interested in Tina but she wasn't aware?"

"Did they spend a lot of time together on the trip?" Harry asked. "Enough that it would have started rumours if everyone hadn't believed that she was interested in Mark?"

"That's a good point," Charles said. "Perhaps she truly was pretending to be interested in Mark so that no one would realise where her interest truly was as Bessie suggested."

"Are we thinking that she told Doug how she felt and he turned her down?" Hugh asked.

"That's certainly one possibility," Andrew replied. His phone buzzed. He glanced at the screen and then smiled.

"I don't suppose that's Nolan with news," Harry said.

"Sadly, it's not. It's something else altogether. Where were we, then? I need to go back to Nolan and tell him to focus on Tina for the next round of questions. Does anyone have anything else to add to what we've already discussed?"

A few people shook their heads.

"I might have more after I read the complete statements, but I doubt it," Harry said. "I can't imagine you missed anything important when you were compiling everything."

"I hope I didn't. I didn't put Tina and Doug together, though," Andrew replied.

"And maybe they weren't together," Bessie said. "It's an angle that needs exploring, though."

"Absolutely," Andrew agreed. He passed out the envelopes full of statements to everyone.

Harry and Charles were quick to exit the room. The others followed more slowly.

"I'm going to take you home and then get an email off to Nolan," Andrew said as he started the car. "And then I have an errand to run. Let's plan on dinner at six, if that's okay with you."

"That's fine," Bessie replied, determined not to ask any questions about the man's errand.

He drove them back to Bessie's. They parted company in the parking area. Inside Treoghe Bwaane, Bessie got herself a glass of water and then sat down with the updated statements. She read through them all twice and then put them down with a sigh.

"There isn't anything there, but I still think Tina killed Doug," she said as she slowly stood up.

She carried the case file up to her office and then locked it in her desk. Then she went and sat on the rock behind her cottage, watching the waves and letting the sea air clear her head. Andrew found her there just before six.

"Did you get the email sent?" Bessie asked.

He nodded. "I just got back from my errand. Give me five minutes to get ready and we can go and get dinner."

"I'll get myself ready, then," Bessie said.

Helen was with Andrew when they knocked on her door a short while later.

"Where do we want to go tonight?" Andrew asked as they walked towards the car.

"What about the pub in the town centre in Ramsey?" Helen suggested. "I loved their food on my last visit."

"That sounds good to me," Bessie said.

A short while later, they were sitting together at a corner table in the small pub. Andrew placed their order at the bar and brought back drinks for them.

"So, my errand," Andrew said after a sip of his drink. "Please don't be cross with me," he said to Bessie.

"Why would I be cross?" she asked.

"Because I was hungry and I wanted to get dinner first."

"Before what?"

Andrew sighed. "The text that I got during the meeting was from the Chief Constable. He has the case file on Joseph Carlson's death ready for us."

Bessie gasped. "He's going to let me take a look at it?"

"He said, considering you work for Scotland Yard, that you can have a look at the file. He also said that he'd gone through it and that there wasn't much of interest in it."

"But you have it?"

Andrew nodded. "I left it in my cottage. It's in a sealed envelope. You can open it as soon as we get back from dinner."

Bessie took a sip of her drink and then looked around the pub. "What's keeping our food?" she demanded.

Helen and Andrew both laughed.

"I'll eat quickly," Helen promised. "And I'll even skip pudding."

"I don't think we have to be in that much of a rush," Bessie said. "I'm excited to read the file, but also a bit reluctant to do so. There's a part of me that thinks I may be happier not knowing what happened to Joseph Carlson."

"We don't have to look at the file," Andrew said.

"Yes, we do," Bessie said firmly.

The food arrived just a few minutes later. Bessie found herself eating far too quickly, so she deliberately put her fork down and took several deep breaths.

"Are you okay?" Helen asked.

"I'm trying not to rush. The food is excellent, but I'm afraid I'm not enjoying it."

"I shouldn't have told you about the file until after dinner," Andrew said. "I simply couldn't stop myself from blurting it out."

After they finished eating, they compromised on pudding by ordering it to take away. Bessie found herself sitting next to Andrew in the car on the way back to Laxey, pressing an imaginary accelerator pedal and wishing the cars in front of them would all disappear.

"Shall I bring the file over to your cottage?" Andrew asked.

Bessie nodded. "I'll put the kettle on. We can have tea and pudding while we read."

"I know I can't see the file," Helen said. "But I truly don't mind. I'll just curl up with my pudding and some telly. Just send Dad home at a reasonable hour."

Bessie laughed. "I'll do my best."

Inside her cottage, she put the kettle on and then changed

into comfortable clothes. She was just putting their puddings on to plates when Andrew knocked.

"That's the entire file?" Bessie asked, looking at the thin envelope that Andrew was carrying.

"That's the entire file, which suggests that it was never a murder investigation."

"I suppose that's good news, really."

She made tea and then sat down at the table with Andrew, who'd opened the envelope and was flipping through the papers that had been inside.

"I'll let you start with the statement from his wife. I'll read the autopsy report, unless you'd rather start there."

Bessie thought for a minute and then shook her head. "I'm really eager to find out more about Joney."

He handed her a few sheets of paper. Bessie took a deep breath and then began to read.

Half an hour later, she'd read everything twice. She looked at Andrew.

"The coroner determined that Joseph tripped over something and fell. When he fell, he hit his head on a large rock and knocked himself unconscious. Sadly, he landed face down in the sea and drowned."

"His wife said that he'd been drinking."

"What else did she say?"

Bessie sighed. "She sounds very young and very scared. They hadn't been married for long. She kept apologising for not going out looking for Joseph. She seems to feel guilty that he was found by someone walking a dog instead of by her."

"Surely she'd noticed that he was missing."

"She claims she didn't realise that he hadn't come back to the cottage." Bessie looked at her notes. "Apparently, Joseph got home from work around six. They had dinner together and then Joseph had a few drinks. Joney left him drinking in the sitting room and went up to the bedroom. The police woke her when they knocked on her door the next morning."

"So she went to bed and Joseph went out for a walk?"

"According to Joney, he often went for walks on the beach late at night." Bessie frowned. "She also said that she thought he might have been meeting someone on the beach, that he sometimes arranged to meet friends out there in the evening."

"Friends?"

"I'm guessing, based on what Joney said, but it sounds as if she thought Joseph was seeing another woman behind her back."

"How long had they been married?"

"Seven months."

"And he was cheating?"

"Joney certainly seemed to think so. You may not agree with my interpretation of her words, of course, but it seems fairly straightforward to me."

"I'll read the reports for myself, just out of interest, but I don't imagine I'll disagree with you."

"Joney also says that Joseph sometimes came back from his walks and just slept on the couch rather than going up to the bedroom."

"They weren't very happy together, were they?"

Bessie shrugged. "It doesn't sound as if they were, but she did rename the cottage after his death."

"Which now feels rather odd."

"I think he had a drinking problem," Bessie said. "Joney mentions that he'd been let go from his last job because he'd been caught drinking at work. He'd started a new job only a few weeks before he died."

Bessie handed him the papers she'd read and then took the rest of the file from him. She read through the coroner's report and the report made by the first constable on the scene. Then she read the witness statement from the man who'd found the body. There were a few other statements in the file, but none of them were of interest to Bessie.

"It seems fairly simple," Andrew said after he'd read the rest of the file. "Joseph drank too much. I suspect he and Joney had a row of some sort. He headed outside for a walk, and she went to bed. If he was drunk and angry, he was probably walking fast and not paying attention to where he was going. Some sections of the beach are very rocky now. I assume they were the same all those years ago."

"The large rocks have all been there since I bought the cottage. From the description in the constable's report, I can picture exactly where the body was found. The hand-drawn map isn't much use."

Andrew chuckled. "It is rather badly done, isn't it? If any photos were taken, they've been lost over the years."

Bessie put her pen down. "I know more than I did, but I still don't know why Joney named the cottage Treoghe Bwaane. Perhaps I need to see if I can find any surviving members of her family. Maybe she married again and had children."

"She might have been pregnant when her husband died."

"I hadn't thought of that, but, of course, you're correct. And if she didn't remarry or have children, maybe her sister had some. I shall have to visit the archives and search though the parish registers to see what I can find."

Andrew gathered up all of the documents and put them back into their envelope. "I shall return this to the Chief Constable and thank him for sharing it with us."

"Yes, please tell him that I'm very grateful," Bessie said.

"And now I should get back to my cottage before Helen starts to worry."

"I do hope that you hear from Nolan again before our next meeting."

"He emailed me earlier to say that he was going to talk to Tina. I haven't heard from him since, but I expect to have a report on that interview before we meet tomorrow."

Bessie walked Andrew to the door and watched as he made his way back to his cottage. He waved before he went inside. Bessie shut and locked the door and then tidied the kitchen. When that was done, she headed up to bed.

"You walked up the stairs a married woman, practically a newlywed, and you woke up a widow," Bessie said as she went up the steps. "It sounds as if you and Joseph had had a fight. Maybe you were hoping that he'd go out and not come back. Or maybe you were sad and lonely and hoping that you'd make up quickly."

Bessie shook her head. "And now I'm talking to myself. I need to go to bed."

CHAPTER 15

When Bessie woke up the next morning, her first thought was about Joney. How must the young woman have felt, waking up to the sound of someone knocking on the cottage door? Maybe she assumed it was Joseph and rushed down to welcome him home. How horrible it must have been for her to open the door and find the police standing there.

Bessie shook her head to try to clear it. Joney's situation was very different from her own, but she couldn't help but think about how devastated she'd been when she'd been told that Matthew was dead. She'd found solace in this small and cosy cottage, but for Joney maybe it was just a constant reminder of the man that she'd lost.

"She didn't sell it for ten years," she said thoughtfully as she got dressed. "And then she sold it to her sister. I wonder why."

Feeling as if she'd never know the answers to any of the questions that kept popping into her head, Bessie went down the stairs and into the kitchen. It was raining and Bessie was feeling oddly cross with the world, so she made herself a bowl of porridge.

She disliked porridge, but she knew it was good for her, so she ate it all with only a few muttered complaints. Then she pulled on her waterproofs and went out for her walk. Andrew was waving from his doorway as she walked back towards home a short while later.

"Have you heard from Nolan, then?" Bessie asked after Andrew had stepped backwards to let her into his cottage.

"I have. There are some things to report. I've already sent back a few additional questions based on what he said, but I'm certain we'll have more to add."

"It sounds as if the investigation is moving forwards, then."

Andrew shrugged. "I hope so. Nolan agrees that he needs to take a closer look at Tina, but as yet there isn't any evidence to back up the idea that she was interested in Doug."

"What did the others say about the idea?"

"Nolan is still typing up those reports. I'll have them for the meeting, but I don't have them yet."

"Are you staying here to watch for emails all morning, then?"

He chuckled. "I don't have to, if you have an idea of something you'd rather do instead."

Bessie shrugged. "It's pouring with rain. Staying inside is probably the best option."

"Hi, Bessie," Helen called as she walked into the sitting room. "I'm going to make pancakes with bacon for breakfast. Would you like some?"

Bessie thought about the porridge that she'd eaten not that long ago. In spite of her healthy breakfast, she found herself saying "yes, please" to Helen's offer. After breakfast,

Helen lent Bessie a book from the stack that she'd brought with her from London. Bessie read happily until midday.

"I'm not terribly hungry," she said when Andrew suggested lunch.

"I shouldn't be, because I had a lot of pancakes, but I'm actually starving. Maybe it's because I've done nothing but pace back and forth while staring at my computer screen all morning."

"Do you want to go out for lunch?"

"Would you mind staying here? I had an email half an hour ago from Nolan, and he promised that I'd have one more within the hour."

"I can make sandwiches and bring them over here," Bessie offered.

Andrew nodded. "That would be great. Helen said something earlier about needing a trip to the shops for some bits and pieces."

"I'll bring enough for her, too," Bessie said.

As she made her way back to Treoghe Bwaane, she was happy to see that the rain had stopped. After making several different types of sandwiches, she put them into a box and added a few packets of crisps, three apples, and two bananas.

Andrew opened the door to her knock. "I just had that last email," he told Bessie. "And things are getting interesting in Pennsylvania."

"Oh?" She frowned. "But you can't tell me anything, can you?"

He shook his head. "It's very nearly time for the meeting. Let's eat and then get over to Ramsey. Maybe everyone will be early."

Bessie laughed. Helen joined them for lunch, and she and Bessie had a lively conversation about the first half of the book that Bessie had been reading.

"Take it home and finish it at your leisure," Helen told her as Andrew cleared the table. "You can give it back to me next month if you don't finish it while we're here this time."

"Thank you. I do want to find out what happens to everyone."

A few minutes later, Bessie and Andrew were on their way to Ramsey. Today Jasper had them meeting in a conference room on the fourth floor.

"This is almost as nice as the penthouse," Bessie said as she and Andrew walked into the room. Large windows gave them a spectacular view of the sea.

"And we have more cake," Andrew said.

Bessie grinned. "The pastry chef must be trying more ideas."

She filled a plate and then sat down with her cake and a cup of tea. Andrew sat down next to her and opened his laptop.

"I didn't get these updates printed," he said. "I'll just tell you what's happening, and we can discuss how to move things forwards from there."

"We just need Tina to confess," Bessie said.

Andrew laughed. "I don't think that's going to happen."

Harry and Charles actually arrived before the others for a change. They both got drinks, and Charles even took a few cake samples. They were just taking seats when John, Doona, and Hugh arrived.

"More cake," Hugh said excitedly. He made careful stacks of the cubes, managing to pile far more on to his plate than Bessie had imagined would be possible.

Doona took a few of each of the samples while John seemed to be focussed on the chocolate options. When everyone was sitting around the table, Andrew smiled at them.

"Nolan has had some interesting conversations with the campers," he said.

"Everyone turned on Tina," Harry guessed.

"In a way, yes," Andrew agreed. "Nolan asked each of them if they thought there was any chance that Tina and Doug were more than friends, or if they'd seen any unusual behaviour between the two of them, either in the days or weeks before the camping trip or on the day they left Pittsburgh."

"I hope he broke it down into multiple questions," Charles said.

"He did, but he summarised their replies for me. He sent full transcripts of the interviews, too, but I don't know that they matter at this point. Let's start with Mark."

Doona laughed. "We always start with poor Mark. It seems especially cruel now, since it seems likely he didn't do it."

"But he had some interesting things to say," Andrew told her. "For a start, he said that he'd always thought that Tina was interested in Doug, right up until everyone started talking about how she was chasing after him."

"Why didn't he tell Nolan that twelve years ago?" Doona asked.

"You're going to wonder that a lot with each interview," Andrew warned her. "Nolan asked Mark that question, though, and Mark said that he would have mentioned it if he'd thought it mattered, but as far as he knew, Tina had given up on Doug and set her sights on him instead."

"And I'm sure he thought that was perfectly logical, since he was such an amazing catch," Doona said dryly.

Andrew shrugged. "Let's say he wasn't surprised. He said something about how nearly all women fell for him eventually, but that he was rather particular about which women he actually encouraged."

"So Mark thought that Tina had formerly been interested in Doug," Bessie said. "What made him think that?"

"Apparently, she used to hang out at the bar a lot, especially when Doug was working, and whenever she was asked to fill in, she always asked whether or not Doug would be there, too," Andrew said. "Mark said he didn't pay much attention because just about everyone who worked there preferred to work with Doug rather than the other two guys who also worked there full-time."

"Did Mark see or hear anything else interesting?" Doona asked.

"He said that on the camping trip, Tina spent a lot of the day hanging around Doug. At the time, Mark thought that she was trying to get Doug to help her find ways to get closer to him, but that was just because everyone kept telling him that Tina was interested."

"Did Tina do or say anything to Mark that made him think that she was interested?" Bessie asked.

"That's just it," Andrew said. "Once Mark really thought about it, he told Nolan that he'd barely spoken to Tina on the camping trip. She'd spent a lot of time with Doug and some time with Patti, but he really saw her only when they were all together in a group."

"It was a small group," Doona said.

Andrew nodded. "But Tina said in her statement that she thought she was making progress towards getting closer to Mark. Mark doesn't remember her doing anything of the kind."

"What else did Mark say?" Charles asked.

"He said that his ego was bruised slightly, but that he was starting to doubt that Tina was ever interested in him, and then he suggested that if Tina was interested in Doug, that maybe he turned her down and she killed him."

"I knew he'd get there eventually," Harry said.

Andrew nodded. "Rusty's take on things was also interesting."

"He was Doug's closest friend. Surely, he'd have known if Tina had made a play for Doug," Doona said.

"When asked about the relationship between Doug and Tina, Rusty said that at one point Doug had mentioned seeing Tina everywhere he went, but that had been a month or more before the murder."

"What did he mean by that?" Bessie asked.

"Apparently, Tina had started shopping at the same shops that Doug regularly used and sometimes seemed to be hanging around the area near Doug's flat. Rusty said that he teased Doug that he'd found himself a stalker, but, after a week or two, Doug stopped mentioning it."

"Doug stopped mentioning it," Bessie echoed. "That doesn't mean that it stopped."

"No, it doesn't. Nolan is going to see if he can track down any of Doug's former neighbours to see if any of them remember seeing Tina in the area in the weeks before the murder, but that might be difficult after twelve years."

"So Tina was stalking Doug in the weeks before the murder," Doona said.

"We don't have any evidence to suggest that was the case," Andrew said quickly. "According to Rusty, not long after Doug stopped talking about the matter, Tina told Rusty that she was interested in Mark. She asked him to help her find ways to get closer to the man."

"And he invited her on the camping trip," Harry said.

"Actually, he denied inviting her. He told Nolan that he didn't really care for her and that if it had been up to him, she wouldn't have been invited, but it wasn't up to him."

"Who made the decisions about whom to invite?" Bessie asked.

Andrew shrugged. "No one seems to be able to answer that question. The most likely answer is that Doug invited Tina to come with them."

"But surely Doug wanted to avoid her," Doona said. "Even if the stalking had stopped, surely he didn't want to spend a weekend with her."

"We may never know the whole story. Rusty claims he didn't invite her. According to Mark, he didn't invite anyone. Doug told him that he and some friends were thinking about going camping and Mark invited himself along, promising to bring tents for everyone if he was included."

"I hope Nolan asked everyone who invited Tina," Doona said.

"There's just Patti left," Andrew said. "And he did ask her. Let me go back a bit, though. When Patti was asked about the relationship between Doug and Tina, she frowned and said that she thought maybe they'd gone out a few times a while back but that things hadn't worked out."

"Based on what?" Bessie asked.

"She said it was just a feeling, based on how Doug and Tina acted when they were together. She said she sometimes saw Tina staring at Doug in a weird way. When Nolan suggested that Tina might have stalked Doug at some point in the past, Patti said that wouldn't surprise her. Then she said that Tina had been practically stalking Mark now that she'd set her sights on him."

"I can't believe none of this came out over the past twelve years," Hugh said.

"They were never asked these exact questions," Andrew replied. "And they were all convinced that Tina was after Mark. It wasn't until that was called into question that they started thinking more seriously about Tina's relationship with Doug."

"So Tina had moved on from stalking Doug to stalking Mark, or that's what Patti seemed to think, anyway," Doona said. "But maybe she was still stalking Doug and only pretending to be interested in Mark. She could sit in the corner of the bar and stalk both of them at the same time most nights, anyway."

"So what did Tina have to say about all of this?" Harry asked.

"She laughed when Nolan asked her about her relationship with Doug. She said that they'd been friends and that they'd worked together at the bar occasionally, and that she thought he was a nice guy. Then she reminded Nolan that Doug's death had ruined her life and insisted that there was no way she'd killed him."

"Is that a summary of the entire conversation, or did she really jump from talking about their relationship to denying that she killed him?" Harry asked.

"She really made that leap," Andrew replied. "Nolan noted it, too."

"Did Nolan ask her about what Rusty had said about her stalking Doug?" Bessie asked.

"Not in so many words. He said that a witness had come forwards to say that he or she had seen Tina hanging around Doug's flat in the weeks before the murder. Again, Tina just laughed and said that after twelve years people's memories do funny things."

"Mark said that she'd spent a lot of the camping trip with Doug. Did the others say the same?" Bessie asked.

"Patti said that she remembered seeing Doug and Tina together that day but that she hadn't paid much attention. She said she'd spent most of the day waiting to see what would happen when Tina made a play for Mark."

"So she was expecting Tina to say something to Mark," Harry said.

Andrew nodded. "And she'd been watching Mark. She said she was pretty certain that he was going to tell Tina he wasn't interested. She said she thought she'd be spending the night trying to calm down a sobbing Tina."

"But it never happened," John said.

"No, and Patti was relieved about that. Rusty said that he wasn't paying attention to where anyone else was on the camping trip. He was simply focussed on enjoying getting away from the city."

"What about…"

Hugh's question was interrupted by the sound of a mobile phone. Andrew made a face.

"That's mine," he said, pulling his phone out of his pocket. "And it's Nolan. I'll just step outside."

"Tina has confessed," Doona said as Andrew walked out of the room.

"I doubt it," Harry said. "I suspect one of the others has remembered something relevant. Now that they have had their attention focussed on Tina, they may remember a lot of interesting things."

"We just have to hope that what they remember actually happened," Charles said.

Harry nodded. "If Tina didn't do it, the killer will be eager to, quote, 'remember,' unquote, all sorts of things that never happened but that will make Tina look more likely as the killer."

Bessie sighed. "A confession would make things a good deal easier."

While they were waiting, Hugh got up and filled another plate with cake samples. Bessie found herself getting a few more herself, more to fill the time than because she wanted more cake. As she nibbled through a square, she realised that she really had wanted more cake.

Andrew walked back in a few minutes later.

"You look happy," Doona said.

"Mark just rang Nolan. Tina wants to see him."

"Tina wants to see Mark?" Bessie checked.

Andrew nodded. "Tina told Mark that they needed to

talk. She said that she could prove that Mark had killed Doug but that she didn't want to do anything to hurt her old friend. She said she'd kept her mouth shut for twelve years but that the police were making her nervous now. She claimed she was afraid that the police were trying to make a case against her now, so she had a proposition for him."

"What sort of proposition?" Harry asked.

"According to Mark, she offered to provide him with an alibi. She told him that she'd tell the police that they spent the night together some distance from the camp. She'd come up with an entire story that she seemed to think was believable and she offered to share it with Nolan if Mark would do the same."

"So she's trying to get herself an alibi," John said.

"It certainly seems that way. Mark said that he needed some time to think about her offer. She's going to come to the bar tonight so that they can talk in person."

"She's going to try to frame him," Hugh said. "She must have something from the scene that she's going to try to plant on him or something."

Andrew nodded. "Right after Nolan talked to Mark, Tina rang him – Nolan, I mean. She told Nolan that Mark had rung her and offered to give her an alibi if she gave him one. She said that she'd told him that she'd come and see him at the bar tomorrow night to talk."

"Tomorrow night?" Doona repeated.

"She didn't expect Mark to ring Nolan, obviously," Harry said.

"Or maybe Mark didn't expect her to ring Nolan," Bessie said. "It's all very complicated."

"Nolan is already putting things into place at the bar. He'll have several plainclothes officers there tonight. He'll be there, as well, but out of sight."

"And we'll all be asleep while it's happening," Bessie said

as she tried to work out the time difference between them and Pennsylvania.

"Indeed," Andrew said. "Although I'm not certain I'll sleep."

They talked for a while longer about what was happening on the other side of the Atlantic, but there was nothing they could really do now except wait and see what happened. Andrew assured them that Nolan would ring him as soon as he had anything to report.

After the meeting broke up, Andrew drove Bessie back to Laxey. They walked on the beach and then sat together at Bessie's, talking about nothing much while trying not to think about the events that were unfolding elsewhere. Helen had been to the grocery shop, so she cooked dinner for the three of them, and then they watched an old movie together until it was getting quite late.

"I don't want to go to bed," Bessie said. "I want to wait with you to find out what happened."

"I'm going to bed," Andrew told her. "Whatever happens, Nolan will have piles of paperwork to fill out after it's all over. He won't ring me until that's done, which probably means tomorrow morning, our time, anyway."

In her bedroom, Bessie tossed and turned for over an hour before she finally fell into a restless sleep.

～

WHEN SHE OPENED her eyes the next morning, she nearly jumped out of bed. Getting ready quickly, she headed down the stairs. When she looked outside, Andrew's cottage was dark. Feeling oddly let down, she made herself some toast and then ate an apple while keeping one eye on Andrew's cottage. With breakfast out of the way, she went out for her walk, but she kept it short and stayed close enough to

Andrew's cottage to watch it the entire time. When she finally gave up and let herself back into her cottage, her phone was ringing.

"Is Andrew up yet?" Doona demanded. "John and I have been up for hours, wondering what happened in Pennsylvania last night."

"His cottage is still dark," Bessie told her.

"We're coming down there. We can't wait here any longer," Doona said.

Bessie put the phone down and then jumped when someone knocked on her door.

"Hugh?"

"I was hoping you might have heard something," he said after giving Bessie a hug.

She shook her head and then grinned. "There's a light on in Andrew's cottage now. Maybe we'll hear something soon."

John and Doona arrived a few minutes later. John parked next to Andrew's car. As the pair got out of the car, another car pulled into the parking area. Bessie was surprised to see Charles and Harry emerge from the second car.

"We didn't want to wait for Andrew to ring us," Harry explained as they approached Bessie. "We thought it would be best to be here."

Bessie nodded. "Now we just have to wait for Andrew to arrive." She invited everyone in, and they all sat together in the sitting room, chatting about nothing while they waited. When someone knocked half an hour later, everyone jumped. Bessie waved them all back into their seats and then went and answered the door.

Andrew was grinning broadly. "I saw all of the cars. Is everyone here?"

Bessie nodded. "I hope you have news for us."

"I do."

She stood back to let him in and then shut the door

behind him. Then she followed him into the sitting room. As soon as they were both seated, Harry spoke.

"What happened?" he asked.

"Nolan set up cameras and microphones. Under Pennsylvania law, both parties in a conversation have to consent to being recorded. Nolan was out of sight when Tina arrived, but there were officers around. When Tina got there, Mark mentioned to her that he'd had security cameras put in throughout the entire building. He actually told her to smile because she was on camera. She just laughed and then said they urgently needed to talk."

"She didn't object to being recorded?" Bessie asked.

"Her lawyers will probably argue that she didn't realise that she was consenting to being recorded, but there were several signs inside the bar that stated clearly that everything in the building was being recorded and monitored. Nolan did say that she kept her voice low when talking to Mark, but he'd put a very sensitive listening device in the vase on the table where they were sitting."

"And what did she have to say?" Harry asked.

"She insisted that she wanted to help him by giving him an alibi. In return, he would be giving her one, of course, but mostly she wanted to help him because she knew he'd killed Doug."

"And what did Mark say to that?" Doona asked.

"He laughed and said he hadn't killed Doug, which made him reluctant to provide her with an alibi. She then claimed that the stress of the investigation was making her sick and asked if they could go up to his flat and talk there."

"Were there cameras there, too?" Harry asked.

"There were. Mark agreed and took her upstairs. Then he said he had to go back down to the bar for a few minutes. When he left her alone, the cameras in the flat clearly showed Tina putting a bloodstained T-shirt into Mark's closet."

Bessie blew out her breath. "She'd kept the T-shirt she was wearing when she stabbed Doug?" she asked.

"She may not have been wearing it," Andrew replied. "As of right now, Nolan suspects that it was one of Doug's T-shirts. He thinks she grabbed it and used it to soak up some of the blood and then took it with her."

"As a souvenir, or because she thought she might use it to frame someone in the future?" John asked.

"One of those," Andrew said. "Or maybe both."

"So she's been arrested for murder," Doona said.

"Right now, she's just being held for questioning, but Nolan was able to get a search warrant for her flat. There he found a sort of shrine to Doug including what he thinks are scraps from the sleeping bag that Doug was murdered in."

"We've solved another one," Harry said.

"Not that I'll ever understand how anyone could kill another human being," Bessie said, "but Tina really didn't seem to have any reason to kill Doug."

"Maybe we'll find out more as the police gather more evidence," John said.

They talked for a while longer before Harry and Charles decided that they needed breakfast. By that time though, it was nearly midday. Bessie offered to cook for everyone, but Charles insisted on taking them all out for lunch to celebrate their success. He and Harry flew back to London the next day, leaving Bessie to enjoy spending time with Andrew and Helen for the remainder of their stay.

ON ANDREW'S LAST DAY, he finally had some additional news from Pennsylvania.

"Nolan rang me last night," he told Bessie as they headed

towards Onchan to get lunch at Dan's restaurant. "As the evidence has been mounting, Tina finally started talking."

"She's confessed?"

"Not exactly, but she has told Nolan all about her relationship with Doug. Rusty was right about her stalking him. Apparently, she fell in love with him the day she met him, and she knew that he felt the same way."

"Too bad Doug didn't know any such thing," Bessie murmured.

"She told Nolan that she divorced her husband immediately because she knew that she and Doug belonged together. Then she started hanging out in all of his favourite places so that she could see him."

"I thought her husband cheated on her."

"Yes, so did I, but, apparently, even if he did, she only left him because she'd fallen in love with Doug."

"But Doug didn't feel the same way."

"She said she knew they were supposed to be together, but she never got the chance to tell him that. Then she decided to try to make him jealous by pretending to be interested in Mark. The day of the camping trip, she asked him to meet her in the third tent so that he could help her find a way to win Mark's heart. When she got there, she said she thought he'd declare his undying love. Instead, he gave her some tips on how to approach Mark."

"So she stabbed him?" Bessie asked.

Andrew shrugged. "She claims that she left him in the third tent and went away to cry. When she got back, she went back to bed. She told Nolan that someone else must have come into the campground and stabbed Doug while she was crying down by the stream."

"And how does she explain the bloodstained T-shirt?"

"Nolan said she just shrugged and then changed the subject. He's pieced it together, though. While she and Mark were waiting for the police to arrive, she went into her tent for a while and then went some distance away, carrying a small shovel. She told Mark that she needed to relieve herself. Obviously, he looked away until she came back. That gave her the opportunity to bury the bloodstained T-shirt and the sleeping bag scraps. Nolan is trying to find someone who saw her when she went back to get the items later."

"Poor Doug."

"Indeed."

Bessie was happy when they reached the restaurant. Dan's amazing cooking and a long conversation with Carol and little Wendy did a lot to lift her spirits.

"I hope next month's case isn't as sad," she said to Andrew as they drove back to Laxey a few hours later.

"I have two cases I'm considering for next month. Would you rather look at another murder or a missing person case?"

Bessie thought for a minute. "We haven't looked for a missing person for a while. That might make a nice change."

"If nothing else comes up between now and then, we'll look for Brent Newton next month, then," Andrew told her as he parked next to her cottage. "For now, let's take a walk on the beach. I ate too much pudding."

"We both ate too much pudding."

THE NEWTON FILE

AN AUNT BESSIE COLD CASE MYSTER

Release date: October 4, 2024

This month the cold case unit has a special guest. Jeremy Harrison is a reporter for a London newspaper, and he's been given special permission to sit in on the cold case unit meetings. He can't be given access to the actual police reports on the case, but this case got a lot of coverage in the newspapers back when it happened. One paper has been doing an annual update on the case, as well, which means Jeremy will have nearly as much information as the actual members of the unit.

That's partly due to the fact that the police files don't give the unit a lot of information from which to work. Brent Newton got into his car one morning and drove away, presumably heading for his office. He never arrived and was never seen again.

Meanwhile, Jasper Coventry, the manager at the Seaview, is worried about another missing person. Adam Meyer checked in but hasn't been staying in his room. Adam's friends aren't concerned, but Jasper finds the entire situation worrying.

Bessie and her friends are going to have to work twice as hard to find two missing people. But as the investigation continues, it seems increasingly unlikely that they are going to get two happy endings.

A SNEAK PEEK AT THE NEWTON FILE

AN AUNT BESSIE COLD CASE MYSTERY

Release date: October 4, 2024

Please excuse any typos or minor errors. I have not yet completed final edits on this title.

Chapter One

"I do hope I'm not late," the man in the doorway said as he walked into the conference room. He appeared to be in his late fifties, with thinning grey hair that had all been combed forwards to try to make it look less sparse. He was wearing a brown suit that seemed to be at least two sizes too big. It was threadbare, and Bessie thought she could see a few stains on the wide lapels as well.

"Not at all," Andrew assured him.

Only ten minutes, Bessie thought.

The man stopped a few steps into the room and slowly looked around. Bessie had to force herself to stare back at him when they locked eyes. Eventually his gaze moved on to

Andrew, who was sitting next to her. Finally he focussed on the table at the back of the room.

"Coffee?" he asked.

Andrew nodded. "Help yourself."

The man walked to the table and poured himself a cup of coffee. "We don't get biscuits like this in the newsroom," he said, picking up a plate and filling it with an assortment of biscuits.

"The hotel's pastry chef made them all himself," Bessie found herself saying. "He's very talented."

"Then he won't stay on the island for long, will he?" the man asked.

Bessie frowned. "Many people love the island and choose to remain here even if they could be very successful elsewhere."

He shrugged. "I can't imagine why. It's been raining since I landed yesterday morning. From what I can tell, there's nothing much to do here. I forgot to pack a few things, and it took me most of yesterday to track down what I needed from all of the different small shops in Ramsey. I had a disappointing lunch in a pub and a barely adequate evening meal at another. I will admit that breakfast and lunch today, both of which I ate here at the Seaview, were much better, but I don't want to have to eat at the hotel for every meal."

"There are some excellent restaurants on the island," Andrew told him. "I can give you a list."

"You'd better give me directions, too," the man replied. "Yesterday I took the wrong exit at a roundabout on my way from the airport to here and I was lost for ages in what seemed to be the middle of nowhere."

"How unfortunate," Bessie murmured.

Doona turned a snort of laughter into a cough.

The man glanced at Bessie and then stared at Doona. She

looked down at the notebook in front of her. Bessie could tell that she was struggling not to laugh.

After an awkward pause, the man walked over and took a seat next to Charles. He put his coffee and his plate on the table and then got out a small recording device.

"I'm going to record this," he announced. "That saves me having to write down every word you all say. It also protects me in case you forget what you told me and decide later that I'm lying or making things up."

Does that happen to you often? Bessie wondered.

"I'm also going to take notes, of course," he continued as he pulled a battered notebook out of another pocket.

Andrew nodded. "Let's start with introductions, then," he said.

The man shrugged. "I read the article that was printed in the local paper here. I know who you all are."

"Maybe you could introduce yourself," Harry suggested.

The man looked surprised and then gave a self-deprecating chuckle. "Yes, of course. I forget that when I'm not in London, I'm not generally recognized. I'm Jeremy Harrison. I'm an investigative journalist based in London."

"Mr. Harrison is here by invitation," Andrew said. "My supervisors at Scotland Yard thought it would be advantageous to the unit if we spoke to him."

Bessie frowned. When Andrew had told her about Jeremy Harrison's impending visit, she'd questioned the logic behind allowing the man to attend their meeting. Andrew had been unable to suggest a single good thing that could be expected to come out of speaking to the man, but he also couldn't say no to his supervisors.

"Oh, but you all must call me Jeremy," the man said, waving a hand. "We're all friends here, after all."

Bessie and Doona exchanged glances. Doona rolled her

eyes and slowly shook her head. Jeremy was busy flipping through his notebook and didn't notice.

"Right, let's save some time, then," Jeremy said. "I'll tell you each what I know about you, and you can correct anything that isn't accurate."

He glanced up and looked around the table. "Okay?" he asked.

A few people nodded. Bessie picked up a biscuit and took a bite, hoping the sugar would improve her mood.

"Andrew Cheatham," Jeremy began. "You started this cold case unit after retiring from Scotland Yard. You've written several books on investigative techniques but chose not to work as a consultant on active cases. Instead, you started a very nontraditional cold case unit made up of former Scotland Yard police inspectors, a few working members of a small island police force, and a pair of seemingly random civilians. I'm sure you had your reasons for selecting the members of the unit. I'm already trying to work them out."

"I'd be happy to explain my choices to you," Andrew told him.

He shook his head. "Maybe, at the end of the week, if I haven't worked it all out for myself."

Andrew frowned. "It isn't complicated. I selected people..."

Jeremy held up his hand. "We can have that conversation another day. Let's move on." He looked around the table and then focused on Harry. "Harry Blake, former homicide inspector with a special interest in the very worst crimes imaginable. You're very much in demand as a consultant. I'm surprised you waste a week each month on this unit. It can't pay anywhere near as much as you can charge for your consulting work."

"The work that this unit does is very satisfying," Harry said.

A SNEAK PEEK AT THE NEWTON FILE

"I'm going to take that to mean that you've managed to catch a few killers," Jeremy replied. "Of course, there have been quite a few cold cases in the news over the past year or so – cold cases that were suddenly solved, that is. I don't suppose you'd care to take credit for the ones that were solved by this unit?"

Harry raised an eyebrow. "If you're asking me, I have no comment."

Jeremy looked at Andrew. "Do you have any comment?"

Andrew shook his head. "We don't discuss our success rate, or our failure rate, with anyone outside of the unit."

"But you can confirm that you've solved at least one or two cases, can't you? I mean, Harry said the work was satisfying. It wouldn't be if you were just going around in circles every month and leaving cases unsolved."

Andrew smiled thinly. "No comment."

Jeremy laughed. "Right, then, let's move on. Charles Morris, retired inspector and respected international expert on missing persons. Again, someone very much in demand as a consultant. I can't imagine the cold case unit looks for missing people very often, so why are you here?"

"Like Harry, I find the work that we do here very satisfying," Charles said in a flat tone.

"Wouldn't it be more satisfying to be in London, being paid a fortune to consult when some billionaire's daughter runs away from home?" Jeremy asked, his tone mocking.

Bessie frowned. She knew that the daughter of a very wealthy man had recently disappeared. The papers had been full of speculation that she'd been kidnapped, and it wouldn't have surprised Bessie to hear that Charles had been asked to consult on the case. When the young woman was found two days later happily sailing on a yacht in the Caribbean, a trip she'd simply forgotten to tell her father she was taking, the press had quickly moved on to other stories.

"Over the months I've been coming here, I've come to appreciate the island," Charles told him.

"And do you look for Mandy everywhere you go?" Jeremy asked.

Charles flushed. "No comment," he said tightly.

"You know she was from the island, right?" Jeremy asked. "She was actually born here, but she and her parents moved to Liverpool when she was three. They moved around a lot after that, too, before Mandy disappeared."

"I think that's quite enough of that," Andrew said.

Jeremy sighed. "I'm simply fascinated by Charles's past. His first girlfriend disappeared under mysterious circumstances. From what I could discover, he's never been involved with another woman. Instead, he…"

Charles got to his feet as Andrew held up a hand.

"I said that was enough," Andrew said sharply. He waved a hand at Charles. "Jeremy is done being rude," he told him.

Charles sat back down, a deep frown on his face. Jeremy gave him a smug smile and then moved his attention elsewhere.

"John Rockwell, police inspector with the Laxey Constabulary. You have your fair share of skeletons, too, but I'll skirt around them so I don't upset anyone else. Your first wife died unexpectedly while on honeymoon with her second husband. No one seems to have come up with a satisfactory explanation for her death yet. She was travelling with a doctor. She should have been safer than most."

John stared at him for a moment. "Do you have any questions for me about my part in the cold case unit?"

Jeremy grinned. "I do. How many times have you been the one who spotted the killer?"

"We don't track that sort of thing here. Everything we do is a team effort," John replied.

"And do you find it very satisfying work, too?"

"I wouldn't keep doing it if I didn't enjoy it," John replied.

"Of course, you still work full-time for the island's constabulary. Has it been difficult, being a part of this team while still working?"

John shook his head. "Not at all."

"I was told that you get time off from your job to attend the unit meetings. Surely that causes jealousy and resentment from the other inspectors who weren't lucky enough to get picked for the unit."

"I've never encountered any such thing," John said.

Jeremy grinned. "Maybe it would be more likely if you were just a lowly constable, working in a team full of world-renowned police inspectors. Hugh, why don't you tell me how that feels?"

Hugh flushed. "Obviously, I'm well aware of what an amazing opportunity and privilege being a part of this unit is. I work hard here, and I never take my place in the unit for granted."

"And how frustrated are the other constables who haven't been given the same opportunity?"

"No one has said anything to me to suggest that anyone is frustrated," Hugh replied.

"I suspect they'll say something to me," Jeremy told him.

"I don't believe you've any reason to interview anyone in the Isle of Man Constabulary," Andrew said.

Jeremy grinned. "I want to get some local colour for the story, though. No one knows the island as well as the constables who patrol it every day."

"If you want to speak to anyone in the Laxey Constabulary, you can arrange it through my office," John said. "Otherwise, my constables have been trained to tell reporters 'no comment' when asked any questions."

"I wasn't planning on conducting formal interviews or

anything," Jeremy protested. "I just wanted a casual chat with a few people. As I said, I want some local colour."

"The fact that the unit meets on the Isle of Man is not at all relevant to what we do," Andrew said.

"Perhaps not, but it's an interesting component of what is a very unusual unit. When I first heard about the unit, I assumed that the meetings were being held in London. Surely that's more logical than having them here."

"Why?" Andrew asked.

Jeremy frowned. "It's London," he said, as if that explained everything.

"Four of the seven members of the unit live on the island," Andrew said. "It is less expensive, therefore, to fly three people here than to fly four to London. Hotels and other expenses are also lower here than they would be in London. We try to do things in the most cost-effective way."

Jeremy shrugged, clearly bored with the turn the conversation had taken. He looked past John and smiled nastily at Doona.

"Ah, yes, Doona Moore. John Rockwell's second wife," he said.

"We aren't married," Doona said.

"Oh, my sources suggested otherwise. Something about a trip to Gretna Green that you two took earlier in the year."

Doona flushed and looked at John. He sighed.

"We are not married," he said flatly.

"And unlikely to be, by the sound of it," Jeremy laughed.

Doona sighed. "Go on, then, be horrible."

Jeremy looked surprised. "I'm not being horrible. Does anyone think that I'm being horrible?"

Bessie nodded.

Jeremy looked at her and narrowed his eyes. "I'm simply repeating things that I've been told by others. What have I heard about Doona, then? John is her third husband, or, rather, he would have been her third husband if she'd married him while they were in Scotland. What were you doing in Gretna Green, if you don't mind me asking?"

"I mind," Doona replied sharply.

Jeremy laughed again. "Touché. I hope you won't be offended if I say that you've been married twice, then. Your first marriage ended in a seemingly friendly divorce. Your second ended when your husband was brutally murdered at the holiday park that he owned. Happily for you, you've now inherited that holiday park, which has made you a very wealthy woman."

Doona snorted. "Check your facts. The park isn't worth all that much, and I only own part of it."

"It was during the investigation into your husband's death that you met Andrew, of course. I understand he was in the holiday cottage next to yours at the park."

Doona nodded. "And he was very kind and helpful during a very difficult time."

Jeremy nodded. "Ah, speaking of happy marriages, Hugh, you and your wife haven't been married for long, have you?"

Hugh frowned. "It's been a few years."

"And you have a little girl called Alice and another baby on the way."

"Her name is Aalish. It's Manx," Hugh said.

"Ah, I see. I understand you didn't have the happiest of childhoods."

"I can't see why that matters," Hugh said.

"I've been told you spent a lot of your teenaged years staying with Bessie," Jeremy continued.

Hugh nodded. "Bessie has always been something of an honorary auntie to all of the children in Laxey. She used to give out good advice with tea and biscuits."

"Except that has all stopped now, hasn't it?" Jeremy asked Bessie.

"It's been a while since I've had a house guest," Bessie admitted.

"Because everyone on the island thinks you're dangerous."

Bessie stared at him for a moment and then laughed. "What a ridiculous notion. Everyone on the island understands that I'm a good deal busier than I used to be now that I'm working with the police on the cold case unit. Out of respect for the work that I'm now doing, teenagers are now less likely to turn up unannounced at my door."

"But a few years ago, Hugh was often at your door?"

Bessie glanced at the young man. To her, he didn't look any older than the teenaged boy who'd spent many nights in her spare bedroom to get away from his parents, who didn't approve of his desire to join the police as soon as he finished school.

"I can't see why any of this matters," Andrew said.

"I want to understand the unit and how it functions," Jeremy told him. "You have to admit that it's an unusual collection of people."

"It's unconventional," Andrew admitted. "But it works."

"How well?" Jeremy demanded.

Andrew grinned. "As I said before, we don't talk about our successes or our failures."

Especially since we've never failed, Bessie thought. *This is case number thirteen for the unit and, so far, we've solved them all. If I were superstitious, I might be worried about this one, but I'm not – not really.*

"At least I'll know how you do this time," Jeremy said with a nasty smile.

"He will?" Harry asked.

Andrew frowned and then nodded slowly. "My supervisors thought it would be interesting for Jeremy to work with us on our case this month. He won't be privy to the police reports, but he'll be given copies of all of the newspaper articles that were printed about the case. We'll discuss the case with him, but we'll have to be careful not to talk about things that we've learned from the police files."

"That's going to be very difficult," Doona said with a frown.

Andrew nodded. "I appreciate that it will complicate things, but my supervisors think it's worth doing anyway."

"It will be interesting to hear Jeremy's thoughts on the case as we work through it," Harry said with an uncharacteristic grin.

Jeremy flushed. "I've been covering the crime beat for decades. I'm fairly certain that I'll be able to provide a lot of interesting insights."

"I've selected a case this month that received a great deal of press coverage," Andrew added. "There's very little in the police files that wasn't released to the press as well."

"That's interesting," Harry said.

"Do you have any questions for anyone before we start talking about the case?" Andrew asked Jeremy.

He nodded. "Elizabeth Cubbon, why is a woman in her eighties – one who has never held down paid employment and who has seen very little of the world – working on a cold case unit with a team of retired police inspectors?"

Bessie inhaled slowly, counting to ten before she spoke. "I'm afraid you'd have to ask Andrew why I was invited to join the unit. Or are you asking why I agreed? I agreed because I've been involved in a great many murder investigations in my life and during some of those investigations, I was able to help the police find the killer. Given the opportunity to be a part of a unit dedicated to solving cold cases and putting criminals into prison was a chance I couldn't pass up."

"Yes, there were rather a lot of murders on the island in a very short space of time. Inspector Rockwell, perhaps you'd care to address why the island's murder rate exploded within weeks of your arrival on the island," Jeremy said.

John slowly shook his head. "I've no idea what drove up the murder rate, but I'm pleased that I can tell you that every case was solved and every killer is now behind bars. The Isle of Man Constabulary works hard to make the island one of the safest places in the world in which to live and work. I wouldn't be raising my children here if I didn't believe the island was safe."

"Ah, yes, your children. Thomas and Amy, right? Thomas is at university now, though. Are you worried about him being in the UK while you're here?"

"All parents worry about their children, whether they are in the next room or living on the other side of the planet," John said.

"At least you still have Amy at home with you. I'm told she looks exactly like her dearly departed mother. Is that one of the things that is coming between you and Doona? Does seeing your daughter every day just remind you of your first true love?"

John chuckled. "You need to do better research," he said. "Quite a lot of that was wrong, but none of it is relevant to the cold case unit, which is what you're supposed to be covering. If you want to gossip about my personal life, there are plenty of people on the island who would love to gossip with you. You can't believe a word any of them say, but they'll all have stories to share, I'm certain."

Jeremy grinned. "Perhaps you'd care to give me a name…"

"Not even a little bit," John replied.

Andrew cleared his throat. "I think we've answered enough of your questions," he said to Jeremy. "Maybe we should focus our attention on the case."

ALSO BY DIANA XARISSA

The Isle of Man Cozy Mysteries

Aunt Bessie Assumes
Aunt Bessie Believes
Aunt Bessie Considers
Aunt Bessie Decides
Aunt Bessie Enjoys
Aunt Bessie Finds
Aunt Bessie Goes
Aunt Bessie's Holiday
Aunt Bessie Invites
Aunt Bessie Joins
Aunt Bessie Knows
Aunt Bessie Likes
Aunt Bessie Meets
Aunt Bessie Needs
Aunt Bessie Observes
Aunt Bessie Provides
Aunt Bessie Questions
Aunt Bessie Remembers
Aunt Bessie Solves
Aunt Bessie Tries
Aunt Bessie Understands
Aunt Bessie Volunteers
Aunt Bessie Wonders

Aunt Bessie's X-Ray

Aunt Bessie Yearns

Aunt Bessie Zeroes In

The Aunt Bessie Cold Case Mysteries

The Adams File

The Bernhard File

The Carter File

The Durand File

The Evans File

The Flowers File

The Goodman File

The Howard File

The Irving File

The Jordan File

The Keller File

The Lawrence File

The Moss File

The Newton File

The Markham Sisters Cozy Mystery Novellas

The Appleton Case

The Bennett Case

The Chalmers Case

The Donaldson Case

The Ellsworth Case

The Fenton Case

The Green Case

The Hampton Case
The Irwin Case
The Jackson Case
The Kingston Case
The Lawley Case
The Moody Case
The Norman Case
The Osborne Case
The Patrone Case
The Quinton Case
The Rhodes Case
The Somerset Case
The Tanner Case
The Underwood Case
The Vernon Case
The Walters Case
The Xanders Case
The Young Case
The Zachery Case

The Janet Markham Bennett Cozy Thrillers

The Armstrong Assignment
The Blake Assignment
The Carlson Assignment
The Doyle Assignment
The Everest Assignment
The Farnsley Assignment
The George Assignment

The Hamilton Assignment
The Ingram Assignment
The Jacobs Assignment
The Knox Assignment
The Lock Assignment
The Miles Assignment
The Nichols Assignment

The Isle of Man Ghostly Cozy Mysteries

Arrivals and Arrests
Boats and Bad Guys
Cars and Cold Cases
Dogs and Danger
Encounters and Enemies
Friends and Frauds
Guests and Guilt
Hop-tu-Naa and Homicide
Invitations and Investigations
Joy and Jealousy
Kittens and Killers
Letters and Lawsuits
Marsupials and Murder
Neighbors and Nightmares
Orchestras and Obsessions
Proposals and Poison
Questions and Quarrels
Roses and Revenge
Secrets and Suspects

Theaters and Threats
Umbrellas and Undertakers
Visitors and Victims
Weddings and Witnesses
Xylophones and X-Rays
Yachts and Yelps
Zephyrs and Zombies

The Margaret and Mona Ghostly Cozies

Murder at Atkins Farm
Murder at Barker Stadium
Murder at Collins Airfield

The Sunset Lodge Mysteries

The Body in the Annex
The Body in the Boathouse
The Body in the Cottage
The Body in the Dunk Tank
The Body in the Elevator
The Body in the Fountain
The Body in the Greenhouse

The Lady Elizabeth Cozies in Space

Alibis in Alpha Sector
Bodies in Beta Sector
Corpses in Chaos Sector
Danger in Delta Sector
Enemies in Energy Sector

The Midlife Crisis Mysteries

Anxious in Nevada
Bewildered in Florida
Confused in Pennsylvania
Dazed in Colorado
Exhausted in Ohio

The Isle of Man Romances

Island Escape
Island Inheritance
Island Heritage
Island Christmas

The Later in Life Love Stories

Second Chances
Second Act
Second Thoughts
Second Degree
Second Best
Second Nature
Second Place
Second Dance

BOOKPLATES ARE NOW AVAILABLE

Would you like a signed bookplate for this book?

I now have bookplates (stickers) that I can personalize, sign, and send to you. It's the next best thing to getting a signed copy!

Send an email to diana@dianaxarissa.com with your mailing address (I promise not to use it for anything else, ever) and how you'd like your bookplate personalized and I'll sign one and send it to you.

There is no charge for a bookplate, but there is a limit of one per person.

ABOUT THE AUTHOR

Diana has been self-publishing since 2013, and she feels surprised and delighted to have found readers who enjoy the stories and characters that she imagines. Always an avid reader, she still loves nothing more than getting lost in fictional worlds, her own or others!

After being raised in Erie, Pennsylvania, and studying history at Allegheny College in Meadville, Pennsylvania, Diana pursued a career in college administration. She was living and working in Washington, DC, when she met her future husband, an Englishman who was visiting the city.

Following her marriage, Diana moved to Derbyshire. A short while later, she and her husband relocated to the Isle of Man. After ten years on the island, during which Diana earned a Master's degree in the island's history, they made the decision to relocate again, this time to the US.

Now living near Buffalo, New York, Diana and her husband live with their daughter, a student at the University at Buffalo. Their son is now living and working just outside of Boston, Massachusetts, giving Diana an excuse to travel now and again.

Diana also writes mystery/thrillers set in the not-too-distant future as Diana X. Dunn and Young Adult fiction as D.X. Dunn.

She is always happy to hear from readers. You can write to her at:

Diana Xarissa Dunn
PO Box 72
Clarence, NY 14031.

Find Diana at: DianaXarissa.com
E-mail: Diana@dianaxarissa.com

Made in the USA
Columbia, SC
07 June 2024